MURDERED BY SUPERSTITION

A Liz Lucas Cozy Mystery - Book 9

BY

DIANNE HARMAN

Copyright © 2018 Dianne Harman

All rights reserved, including the right to reproduce this book, or portions thereof, in any form without written permission except for the use of brief quotations embodied in critical articles and reviews.

Published by: Dianne Harman
www.dianneharman.com

Interior, cover design and website by
Vivek Rajan

This is a work of fiction. Names, characters, places, and incidents either are the product of the author's imagination or are used fictitiously, and any resemblance to actual persons, living or dead, business establishments, events, or locales, is entirely coincidental.

ISBN: 978-1722114664

CONTENTS

Acknowledgments

Prologue

1	Chapter One	1
2	Chapter Two	6
3	Chapter Three	12
4	Chapter Four	20
5	Chapter Five	25
6	Chapter Six	30
7	Chapter Seven	38
8	Chapter Eight	43
9	Chapter Nine	49
10	Chapter Ten	53
11	Chapter Eleven	56
12	Chapter Twelve	59
13	Chapter Thirteen	65
14	Chapter Fourteen	71
15	Chapter Fifteen	74
16	Chapter Sixteen	78
17	Chapter Seventeen	83
18	Chapter Eighteen	87

19	Chapter Nineteen	95
20	Chapter Twenty	98
21	Chapter Twenty-One	102
22	Chapter Twenty-Two	108
23	Chapter Twenty-Three	111
24	Chapter Twenty-Four	115
25	Chapter Twenty-Five	119
26	Chapter Twenty-Six	122
27	Epilogue	128
28	Recipes	131
29	About Dianne	136
30	Surprise!	137

ACKNOWLEDGMENTS

To Tom, Vivek, and Connie, thank you for making me look good! And to you, my loyal readers, thanks for giving me a reason to write!

Win FREE Paperbacks every week!

Go to www.dianneharman.com/freepaperback.html and get your FREE copies of Dianne's books and favorite recipes immediately by signing up for her newsletter.

Once you've signed up for her newsletter you're eligible to win three paperbacks. One lucky winner is picked every week. Hurry before the offer ends!

PROLOGUE

Nicole Rogers stepped off the scale at her fitness center and smiled. *One hundred fifty-one pounds. That's a personal best. I did it! The surgery, the shrink, the workouts — all worth it now.*

She turned and admired her reflection in the mirror. She saw a tall auburn-haired woman with generous lips and large green eyes. After all the years of being fat, she had a hard time identifying with the polished, attractive woman who looked back at her. She turned away from the mirror and opened her locker. Something fell out of it. She bent over to pick it up and held it in the palm of her hand. It was a small wooden doll, put together with clumsy detail, right down to the strands of red wool stuck onto its tiny little head, where clumps of glue were still visible.

"Nicole, are you all right? You look awfully pale," Judy, the woman whose locker was next to hers said. She reached over and put her hand on Nicole's arm. "Maybe you should sit down for a minute. Here, let me help you."

Nicole allowed Judy to steer her towards the wooden bench in the center of the locker room and stared down at the doll she was holding in her hand, a stunned look on her face. The green dots that were the doll's eyes seemed to look back at her.

"Mind if I take a look at it?" Judy asked, sitting down beside her on the bench.

"No, here," Nicole said, handing the doll to her.

Judy turned it over and looked at it. The doll was no more than three inches high, wrapped in a scrap of fabric for a dress. All of the detail was focused on its face, and whoever had made it had gone to a lot of trouble to make it resemble Nicole, right down to the exaggerated drawn-on lips. "That looks like something I saw recently in a magazine. I think it was called a voodoo doll. I kind of remember it from when I went to New Orleans with my parents when I was a kid. We went to some museum, and they had several of them on display. Is this a voodoo doll?"

Nicole nodded. "Yes, but why would someone put a voodoo doll in my locker? In Louisiana, where I grew up, if you got one of these it meant someone wanted to hurt you or kill you." Her chin wobbled and her eyes were bright with unshed tears.

"I don't know much about them," Judy said, pulling out a torn piece of paper that was sticking out from under the fabric. "Hate to tell you this, but your name's written on this piece of paper that was attached to the doll. Maybe someone's playing a joke on you. Can you think of anyone who doesn't like you that would have access to the gym?"

"No," Nicole said, her hand trembling as she took the doll back from Judy. "I can't imagine what this is about."

Judy's eyes displayed her concern as Nicole stood up. "Nicole, you're shaking. Are you going straight home?"

Nicole nodded. "Yes, I think I'm too upset to do anything else." She hesitated before continuing. "What if someone is waiting for me outside? I'm really scared. This isn't the first one of these that I've gotten."

Judy was taken aback. "What do you mean?" she asked.

Nicole's hand was still shaking as she tried to put on her lipstick. "I've found them in my mailbox, in my desk drawer at work, and even in the glove compartment of my car. Like I said, I'm from Louisiana, and I know what getting a voodoo doll means."

"Let me look at it again," Judy said, walking across to where Nicole was standing by the mirror. The doll was on the counter beside her and Judy turned it over in her hands several more times before addressing Nicole. "Did the others have all of these pins stuck in their necks?"

Nicole's eyes were fixed on the mirror, and she nodded as she continued to apply her lipstick. "Yes, I'm pretty sure they did. Actually, I think I've got one of them in my purse." She pulled out a white miniature figure, this one made of Styrofoam, and handed it to Judy.

"Do you mind if I take both of them? I'd like to see what I can find out about voodoo dolls like these."

"Feel free to, I really don't want anything to do with them," Nicole said with a flick of her hand, before placing her lipstick in her gym bag and zipping it closed.

"Nicole, I'm dressed." Judy said as she lifted up her gym bag. "Let me walk you to your car. You have my cell phone number. When you get home, go directly into your house. Lock the door and call me. You might want to think about getting a bodyguard."

Nicole looked at her, wide-eyed. "Are you kidding? Do you think it's that serious? Do you think someone really wants to hurt me? I've never done anything to anyone."

Yes, the dolls were an annoyance, but surely nothing more dangerous than that. Nicole's usual way of dealing with problems was to ignore them until they went away, and it had been her experience, that most of the inconsequential stuff, like these dolls, did just that.

Judy sighed. "I have no idea how far a person is willing to go with this, but it looks like you definitely have someone who would like to see you harmed."

Nicole's expression faltered. This stupid doll thing had gone on for long enough. She decided to talk it over with Cody later, to see what he thought she should do.

"Just think about it," Judy said, as they made their way to their cars in the parking lot. "There's no harm in being careful."

*****

When she got home, Nicole pulled into the driveway of her house, wishing she'd taken the time to clean out her garage, so she could just drive into it, rather than having to get out of her car and walk to her front door, where she would be exposed and out in the open.

It was a short-lived regret, because it was the last thought she had before a steel wire snapped around her neck. She struggled for a few moments, as she unsuccessfully tried to breathe. Her lifeless body went limp, and as the pressure from the steel wire was released, she fell to the ground. Her attacker pulled her body to the far end of the porch where it would not be visible from the street.

CHAPTER ONE

After she left the fitness center, Judy returned to the cottage where she was staying at the Red Cedar Lodge and Spa which was owned by her friend, Liz Lucas. Judy liked to come to the spa every six months or so and see if she could pick up any ideas for the hotel and spa she owned in Calistoga, California. Two years earlier she'd joined the upscale fitness center about a mile from the Red Cedar Lodge to augment the facials and massages she got while staying at the spa.

Usually she felt re-energized when she returned to the cottage at the end of the day, but not this evening. The incident with Nicole had been unsettling, and although she and Nicole were only casual friends, she couldn't shake the gnawing feeling she had of some sort of impending danger.

She remembered Nicole had given her a card with her cell phone number on it the day before, suggesting they get together for lunch at Gertie's Diner for a hamburger. Gertie's was known as far away as San Francisco for having the best hamburgers in Northern California.

Judy opened her purse, took out the card, and punched in the number on her cell phone. She was immediately switched to a recorded message, which she thought was unusual, since Nicole had told her earlier, when they were working out together, that she planned on spending a quiet evening at home and finishing the book she was reading.

She looked at the clock on the nightstand and realized she needed to change clothes if she didn't want to be late to the evening dinner at the lodge, a meal she always looked forward to. Her friend, Liz, was a great cook, and even though Judy had previously been more of a "using the oven as an additional storage area for purses and shoes," sort of woman, now that she owned the Calistoga spa and had a cook who fixed the meals for her guests, the food Liz prepared had become important to her for reasons other than enjoyment. She was always looking for new things that could be added to her spa's dinner menus.

*****

Liz opened the oven to see how the two large stuffed pork loins were doing, and decided they were coming along a little faster than she wanted. She turned the heat down, and then she opened the bottom oven and reversed the pan that held the garlic roasted tomatoes which were resting on a bed of rosemary.

Looks good. Salads are ready, soup's simmering, and the appetizers are on the table in the great room. I'll put the rolls in a few minutes before we eat. Since some of the guests in the cottages have told me they came here for the food based on what their friends told them, I guess I've developed a reputation I better live up to. Don't think anyone will find fault with the sticky toffee pudding cake for dessert. Every time I've served it, someone has asked for the recipe.

"Thought I'd find you in here," Judy said as she walked into the kitchen. "Got a minute to talk to me before the guests arrive?" Her big brown eyes showed concern.

"Of course." Liz removed her oven gloves and set them on the countertop. "You look worried, Judy. What's happening?"

Judy told her about Nicole and the voodoo doll, then she opened her purse and handed the doll that had fallen out of Nicole's locker to Liz. "I know you're going to New Orleans the day after tomorrow. I was wondering if you could kind of ask around and see what you could find out about voodoo dolls, like this one."

Liz peered down at the doll. She'd never seen anything like it before. If it didn't look so sinister, she would have dismissed it as a child's toy. "I suppose I could, but I don't have much to go on."

"Liz, I'm really worried about Nicole." Judy's brow creased. "I didn't want to tell her how serious this doll incident could be, particularly coupled with the picture of the skull and crossbones and the word Bacalou written on another doll which she told me someone put on her front porch last week."

Liz raised an eyebrow, clearly intrigued.

"When I was a child my parents and I went on a trip to New Orleans," Judy continued, "and we visited some museum that was all about this kind of voodoo stuff. I've never forgotten it. I had nightmares for months afterwards. I can't imagine anyone wanting to harm Nicole. From the little I know about her, she seems to have really made some major changes in her life. She's come so far, it doesn't seem fair that someone would want to hurt her or even do something worse to her. Take a look at this doll and tell me what you think."

"This is the one that fell out of her locker?" Liz asked, as she looked at the stick doll again. The longer she held it, the more she had a sense that something was very, very wrong. "It's creepy, I'll grant you that."

"Yes," Judy said, "that's the one that was in her locker. Although I have nothing to base this on, I'm worried about her. She told me this wasn't the first doll she'd found. Nicole's from Louisiana and was familiar with them. She said some of them had pins that had been stuck in the neck as well. I don't know her all that well, but it makes me nervous that she didn't answer her phone when I tried to call her a little while ago. It's probably nothing, just a joke someone's playing on her, but..."

The longer Liz held the doll, the more concerned she became. When Liz and Judy had been in Bellingham, Washington, a few years earlier, Liz had heard a little voice warning her of impending danger.

She'd listened to the voice and because she'd listened to it, she'd been able to save a number of people's lives. Judy was with her and she remembered telling Judy about the voice at the time, but tonight was the first time she'd heard it since then. *"Tell Nicole to be very careful,"* the little voice said. *"Someone is trying to kill her."*

Liz tried to ignore the little voice and the uneasiness that had washed over her, but it didn't work. Once again, she heard the voice saying, *"Tell her to be very careful. Someone is trying to kill her."*

"Liz, what is it? You're as pale as a ghost," Judy said.

"Judy, do you remember when we were in Bellingham, Washington after those horrible facials we had, and a little voice inside me kind of told me what to do and warned me?"

"Yes, I remember it well. I haven't heard you mention it for quite a while. Are you hearing it now?" Judy asked as her eyes narrowed.

"Yes, and it's telling me that Nicole needs to be very careful, that someone is trying to kill her."

Judy let out a gasp. "Oh, Liz, no. That's just horrible. What can we do?" She took the doll back from Liz and returned it to her purse.

Liz shrugged. "At the moment, nothing. All the cottages are full, and the guests will be here for dinner in a few minutes, as well as some people who aren't even staying in the cottages. As the spa's reputation has grown, so has the number of requests from people wanting to come to dinner."

"Liz, you do yourself a disservice. You're one of the best cooks around, and I'm not at all surprised that they're coming for your dinner, but that still doesn't help us with Nicole."

"I know." Liz made a decision. "Judy, I think we should go over to her house after dinner. I wish Roger was here so he could go with us, but he's spending a couple of nights in San Francisco. He has a bunch of client meetings at his law firm, and it just made more sense for him to stay in the city rather than trying to commute back and forth."

"Thanks, Liz. That would make me feel much better if we went over to Nicole's house after dinner. She was having car trouble last week, so I picked her up at her house and took her home a couple of times after working out at the fitness center. I can easily find it again."

The sound of chattering voices reached them from the great room.

Judy smiled at Liz. "I think your first guests have arrived."

CHAPTER TWO

"Liz, you really have become a superb chef, definitely a notch up from a cook," Judy said later on the drive to Nicole's home. "That was a pretty impressive dinner. As a matter of fact, I went into the bathroom and wrote the menu down. I want to give it to my cook and see if she can duplicate it."

Liz smiled. "Thanks, but I'm hardly a chef. I don't have any credentials for that. I just like to cook tasty and interesting food. The good thing is that people seem to like my cooking. I told you I'm going to New Orleans day after tomorrow for a few days to a cooking school. I love the New Orleans style of cooking, and I'd like to learn more about it from some people who know what they're doing."

"I'm envious. I'd love to do something like that."

"Judy, you have the money, and you've told me that your hotel and spa business has gotten to the place where it's practically running itself because of the manager you hired." Liz glanced sideways at her friend. "Why don't you come with me? I called the cooking school last week just to see if there was anything special I needed to bring with me, and they told me they still had several openings. I'd love for you to join me. You mentioned you'd been to New Orleans when you were a child. Have you been back since then?"

"No, and it's been on my list of things to do." Judy's face broke into a grin. "I guess there's no time like the present. I'd love to go with you if I can get airline tickets and confirm that they still have an opening at the cooking school. I'll call the airlines when I get back to the cottage tonight and first thing tomorrow morning, I'll call the cooking school. You'll have to give me their contact information."

"Not a problem. I've done a lot of research on New Orleans, and in addition to learning a lot of stuff about that style of cooking, we'd have fun. Plus, we can see if we can find out anything about the voodoo dolls that have been delivered to Nicole."

Some would say that researching voodoo in connection with a murder is not their idea of fun.

*****

Judy pointed in the direction of a cluster of pretty single-story homes on a quiet tree-lined street. "Nicole's house is the one with no lights on and the gray car in the driveway. It's pretty early, but maybe she's gone to bed. She told me she was in the middle of a good book and planned on reading tonight. Guess it put her to sleep."

"I'll park behind her car, and we can knock lightly on her door. I don't want to scare her if she is asleep," Liz said, pulling into the driveway.

She and Judy got out and walked past Nicole's car on their way up the steps to the front door. Judy knocked lightly on the door and waited. "If it was me and someone had been scaring me with voodoo dolls," she said, turning to Liz, "I'd leave the porch light on, but each to their own." They stood there for several minutes, but no one came to the door.

"It looks like she didn't draw the blinds on the front window," Liz said, looking around. "I'll walk over and see if there's a light on in the back of the house." She walked the length of the porch and screamed as she turned the corner. "Judy, come here. Is this Nicole?"

Judy came rushing over and looked to where Liz was pointing. "Oh no!" Her hand flew up to her mouth. "Yes, that's her. Do you think she's alive?" They were both looking at the body of a woman lying on the porch, a piece of wire tightly wrapped around her neck. Liz bent down and put her fingers on the woman's cold wrist. She looked up at Judy with a sad shake of her head. "There's no pulse and her skin is cold and clammy. I think she's been dead for several hours."

"It's all my fault," Judy exclaimed. "I should have gone home with her. I'm probably the last person to see her alive, because I walked her out to her car."

Liz straightened up. "Judy, there's no way you could have known what was going to happen. No one would have done anything other than what you did. And, you're not the last person to see her alive. That would be the killer."

Judy saw something a few feet from Nicole's prostrate form and walked past the body, pointing to the ground. "Liz, look at this. It's a doll, just like the one I showed you earlier, the one that fell out of her locker." She opened her purse and took out the doll, so she could compare it with the one lying on the porch next to Nicole's body.

Liz walked over to where Judy was standing and looked down at the doll in her hand. She turned to Judy and said, "When I was getting ready for my trip and researching New Orleans, there was a lot of information about voodoo dolls, and these sure look like what I saw. As much as it pains me to do this, I need to call Seth, the chief of police. I don't think he'll have a clue what a voodoo doll is, but since it's here at the scene of the crime, I think we better leave it alone."

She raked a hand through her hair. "Unfortunately, that little voice I heard was right. Someone definitely had it in for poor Nicole. I find the voodoo doll connection really interesting. Like I said, I doubt if Seth will know anything about it, and I doubt that many people here would know about it either. I wouldn't have, if I hadn't done so much research on New Orleans." She looked down at the little wooden doll on the porch, noticing that it had a piece of wire wound around its neck.

"Judy, the doll that you have in your hand, the one that fell out of Nicole's locker, has pins in its neck, right?"

"Yes, why?"

Liz bent down to view the doll better, without touching it. "Look closer at this one. It has a piece of wire wound around its neck and there aren't any pins. Wonder if the pins were a warning, and when the murder was complete, whoever did it used the same wire on the doll that was used on Nicole."

Judy shivered. "I have no idea. This is all completely new to me, and probably will be to pretty much everyone else. Isn't Seth the guy you think is a complete idiot?"

"You've got that right." Liz chuckled softly. "He's the chief of police of Red Cedar, or more accurately described as a bumbling idiot who cares more about giving out speeding tickets than solving murders, but like it or not, he is the chief of police, duly elected by the citizens of Red Cedar."

Liz took off her coat and placed it over Nicole's lifeless form. She didn't know why but it felt like the right thing to do. Then she placed a call to Seth. A moment later he answered, "Chief of Police Seth Williams here, how may I help you?"

"Seth, it's Liz. I'm standing next to a woman who's been murdered. Here's the address." She reeled it off.

"Lady," Seth said, "seems like every time I talk to you there's been a murder. Who is it this time?"

"A woman by the name of Nicole," she looked at Judy who mouthed the word 'Rogers'. "Her last name is Rogers. When will you be here?"

She could hear Seth huffing and puffing on the other end of the line. "Well, I was fillin' out some pretty important forms for the city council on how many speedin' tickets we handed out this week. They'll be reviewin' my salary at their meeting this comin' week, and I wanna' look good, but I suppose a murder is more important."

"I would think it would be, especially to the victim," Liz said drily.

"My deputy and me oughta' be there in about ten minutes. Just hang tight 'til we get there."

"Seth, I wasn't planning on doing anything else." She ended the call with a roll of her eyes.

Judy had been listening to the conversation and shook her head. "You were right. The guy does sound like an idiot."

Nearly twenty minutes later Seth and his deputy arrived, followed a few minutes later by an emergency medical services ambulance and a coroner's van. In the meantime, Seth took Liz and Judy's statements. When he started to pick up the voodoo doll, Liz put her hand on his arm. "Seth, that may have some fingerprints on it. You probably shouldn't pick it up. It could be evidence."

"Liz," he said as he pushed out his chest and pulled his pants up over his spreading belly, "I'm the expert here, if you don't mind me sayin' so, not you. This ain't nothin' but a little doll. Don't mean nothin' at all. Probably was some good luck charm she carried, and it fell outta' her purse. Here, you're so hot and bothered about it, you take it." He handed it to Liz who exchanged a silent look with Judy and put it in her purse.

Seth's deputy cordoned off the area with yellow tape and took photos. When he was finished the coroner took the body to the city mortuary. An off-duty deputy arrived to dust for fingerprints and gather DNA evidence.

"Liz, you and yer' friend can take off," Seth barked in an officious tone of voice. "Better leave this to people who know what they're doin'. Shouldn't take too long. Probably some guy she turned down. That's usually what these things are, just a domestic dispute that got out of hand, or neck, in this case." He laughed, a heartless roar that grated Liz's nerves. "Get it, Liz, neck, not hand?"

Liz looked at him without responding and walked to her car, Judy right behind her.

CHAPTER THREE

Liz and Judy were in a somber mood on their drive back to the lodge.

"Judy, why don't you come to the lodge with me before you go to your cottage. I'll give you the information about the cooking school, and quite frankly, I'm curious about Nicole. If we're going to look into voodoo dolls, I think I should know more about her. And I can practically guarantee you that whatever we do will be more than Seth is going to do. The only thing he wants to do is get back to filling in those traffic violation forms, so he can get his pay raise."

Liz parked her car, and together the two women walked into the lodge. "I'll make some coffee," Liz said. "I think we could both use a cup, unless you'd like something stronger."

"As a matter of fact, I would. There's something about seeing dead people that gives me the jim-jams." Judy shuddered. "How about a little brandy? As much of a gourmet cook as you are, I'm sure you've got some around here somewhere."

"I do, and I'll get you some, but the jim-jams? What is that?" Liz asked, bemused.

"It's kind of like the heebie-jeebies, but I like the term better. While you're getting the brandy, I'll see if I can make a plane reservation." Judy reached into her purse and looked back up at Liz.

"I left my phone in my cottage. Be back in a minute."

A few minutes later, Judy walked into the great room, smiling broadly. "Well, if the cooking school will have me, I'll be in business. I was able to make a reservation on your flight, but they only had one seat available and it was in first class, so I took it."

"Here's a snifter of brandy, Judy." Liz handed a wide glass containing a healthy measure of brandy to Judy. "I guess that means I won't see you from the time we take off from San Francisco until we get off the plane in New Orleans. Right?"

"That's right." Judy took a sip of the brandy and grinned. "I'll be up in the front of the plane drinking champagne with wealthy, handsome men and eating gourmet food. It's a tough life, but someone has to do it. Hope you enjoy your peanuts and pretzels. I might even save a snack for you," Judy said in a teasing voice.

"Thanks, Judy, but I think I'd rather save the stomach space for beignets and pralines when I get to New Orleans," Liz said laughing. There was a pause before Liz broached the subject about the elephant in the room. "To something far more serious. What do you know about Nicole?"

Judy thought for a moment. "We met at the gym and had never gotten beyond the usual chitchat, apart from when we had lunch one day at Gertie's Diner, when she opened up to me. From what she told me, she'd had a pretty tough life, but had really turned it around in the last year or so. That's when she came to Red Cedar from a small town outside of New Orleans."

"That's probably why I didn't know her. Although I don't know everyone in town, still, it is a small town. Even if I didn't know her, you'd think I would have recognized her, but I didn't," Liz said, wincing at the recollection of Nicole's body sprawled on the porch.

"Nicole told me she'd been fat when she lived in the South," Judy said, "and she'd decided to have surgery to get rid of it. Think she called it a stomach-stapling procedure. She said her surgeon insisted she go to a psychiatrist to make sure she was psychologically healthy enough to go through with the surgery.

"The way she described it, her father had left her mother and instead of letting her feelings go, she stuffed her feelings inside while at the same time she was stuffing her face with food. She said her mother, sister, and her had no money, and they were dirt poor. Her mother worked two jobs just to feed her sister and her. She said part of her weight gain came from the cheap take-out food they ate all the time."

Judy took another sip of her brandy, and Liz waited for her to continue.

"Nicole told me she was smart and even though they were dirt poor," Judy went on, "she'd been able to get a scholarship to Tulane University in New Orleans. She told me it was kind of surreal. She'd ride a bus for an hour to get to Tulane, be with a lot of wealthy students, and then take the bus back to some little town."

"Poor thing," Liz said thinking of how easy she and Joe, her previous husband who had died from a heart attack, had made life for their children. She had a lot of admiration for people who had made it through adverse circumstances to make a different life for themselves.

"Fortunately for her," Judy continued, "after she graduated from Tulane, she was able to get a very good job at a bank in New Orleans. She stayed with them for quite a few years and eventually worked her way up to manager. About the time she was debating having the surgery, she noticed in a trade journal there was an opening for a bank manager in Red Cedar, which would be available in six months."

"I think I remember seeing something in the newspaper last year about one of the bank managers retiring," Liz said.

Judy nodded. "Right. Nicole told me that the bank seldom listed openings that far in advance, but they thought no one would want the job in a town as small as Red Cedar, so they listed it with lots of lead time. She didn't want to stay in New Orleans and have everyone notice her weight loss and have to deal with people talking about her, so she applied for the job, was hired, and had the surgery."

"It must have been hard for her to leave her sister and her mother, after all they'd been through," Liz surmised.

"I got the feeling that wasn't the case. She told me that her mother had died from cancer, and she mentioned that she and her sister were not close at all. She said her sister really resented her going to college and getting a good job. Evidently her sister never finished high school and was very jealous of her. She got married when she was very young, and her husband was unemployed most of the time. Her sister supported them by working in a small gumbo diner."

Liz set her glass down on the side table. Several sips of brandy were enough to relax her, but she didn't want the rest of it, and wished she'd stuck with her first choice for a nightcap, coffee with a splash of milk. "Nicole sounds like she was a very interesting person. How did you meet her?"

"Every time I've come to stay at your spa for the last couple of years, I go to that fitness place I joined here. I met her when I was here last year. She'd only been in Red Cedar a few weeks, and she was still a little heavy. She told me the hardest thing she ever did, next to having the surgery, was to walk into a workout facility with a lot of gym rats. I admired her, and we became friends after that."

"Poor thing. I can't imagine anyone going through what she must have gone through, and on her own, without any support from friends or family. It seems hard to believe that someone can make those changes. Yeah, listen to me. As you know, when my husband Joe died unexpectedly several years ago, I had to make some major changes in my life, so scratch what I just said. Guess sometimes we're given new beginnings, and sometimes they're forced on us. Mine were forced. She made her own, but that doesn't always make it any easier," Liz said.

"Well, I for one, was pretty happy to see you back among the living. Particularly after you met and married Roger. Nice to know you had a second chance," Judy said, swirling the remains of her brandy around in her glass, "but it looks like Nicole didn't."

"Judy, it sounds like her life was going well up until now. What do you make of the doll and the skull and cross bones, as well as the pins and then the wire? Did she ever mention whether or not she had any enemies?"

"No." Judy shook her head emphatically. "She told me she was pretty much of a loner because of her weight. She even said she didn't have enough friends to have any enemies. I thought that was a pretty sad statement. She seemed baffled by why she'd gotten the dolls. Having lived in the New Orleans area where voodoo dolls are pretty common, she was aware of what they meant. She said that someone must have wanted to harm her. I just remembered that she gave me the doll she found on her front porch last week. Let me get that one for you as well." She opened her purse and a moment later, handed a doll to Liz.

Liz spent some time looking at the doll. She turned it over, noting its resemblance to a mummy. The doll's head appeared to be a Styrofoam ball wrapped with yarn. Two sticks in the form of a cross formed the body with yarn and twine wrapped around it for clothing. The eyes were buttons which had been glued on. It looked like something a child would make in a pre-school or kindergarten art class.

A small piece of paper with a picture of a skull-and-crossbones had been glued on it, and the word "Babalou" had been written across the top of the paper in block letters with what appeared to be a heavy black marker.

Liz raised her head and looked at Judy. "I don't know what to make of this. I've heard of voodoo dolls and things like that, but I really know nothing about it. When I was researching New Orleans, I ran across an article about a museum in New Orleans that specializes in that type of thing. Since we'll be staying in the French Quarter, and that's where the museum is located, I think we need to go there and see what we can find out. We definitely should take these dolls with us."

"I agree. Like I told you when we were on Nicole's porch, I went to a museum that sounds a lot like the one you just described when I was a child with my parents. Maybe it's the same one." Judy gazed at Liz. "To change the subject, Liz, you look like you're deep in thought. What is it?"

"Well, from what little I've read, it seems that anything related to voodoo is almost always done by someone who knows the person that receives a voodoo doll. From what Nicole told you that would pretty much be the bank people and her sister."

Judy paused while she considered what Liz had said. "I think she told me she hadn't talked to her sister in over five years. She said they had absolutely nothing in common. Nicole mentioned that her sister was quite beautiful, and she thought her sister was embarrassed to have a sister like Nicole who was so fat and unattractive. Why, do you think her sister could be behind this?"

"I have no idea. I'm simply trying to come up with people who might want to harm her. If her sister was beautiful, as Nicole told you, maybe she felt threatened by Nicole losing weight and becoming attractive. I wonder if she's been to Red Cedar. You probably don't know her name, and I have no idea how we'd even begin to go about finding it…"

She was interrupted by Judy, "Actually, I do remember her name because everyone knows that name. Nicole and I even talked about it. Her name is Marie Laveau. That's the name of the 19th century woman who was the voodoo queen of New Orleans."

"Judy, that's downright bizarre. Why would anyone name their daughter that?" Liz asked.

"From what Nicole told me, that wasn't her given name. When her sister became eighteen she legally changed her name to Marie

Leveau."

Liz exhaled. "This whole thing seems a little too convenient for me. Nicole finds voodoo dolls, and her sister has taken the name of a voodoo queen. Then Nicole is murdered. I'm not discounting that it could be her sister, but I don't think anyone whose name is Marie Leveau would leave a trail that easy to follow. Almost sounds to me like someone wanted people to think that."

Judy sat up with a jolt. "Liz, I remember something else she told me. She was concerned because she had to fire a woman shortly after she became the manager of the Red Cedar bank branch. She told me the woman was very angry about it and blamed Nicole, even though the manager before Nicole, as well as Nicole, had found her to be totally incompetent." She tilted her head before continuing.

"I recall asking Nicole if she ever heard from the woman, and she told me she'd called her a couple of times after she'd been fired and found out she'd moved to Colorado to be with her family. Nicole said she'd received a recommendation request from a bank in Denver, and she'd given the woman a very good letter of recommendation, because she had applied for a low-level secretarial job. Nicole felt she'd be fine doing secretarial work, but she certainly wasn't qualified for a management position."

"Hmm." Liz twisted a strand of her hair around her finger. "I wonder if anyone from the bank stayed in touch with the woman? Did Nicole mention if she got together socially with anyone?"

"I think so. One time she introduced me to a woman she called the assistant manager. She'd brought her to the fitness center as a guest. As I recall, her name was Maddie. Maybe she'd know something. I'm sure I can find out."

"Okay, the only other thing I can think of is some kind of romantic relationship that went south," Liz said. "I wonder if you could call Maddie at the bank, and we could have lunch with her? Maybe we could find something out before we go to New Orleans. I really would like to know if Nicole was seeing anyone. Why don't you call her first thing in the morning and ask her to meet us at Gertie's? Gertie knows everything that's happening in town anyway, so she probably already knows about Nicole's death, but why don't you call Maddie in the morning?"

"Will do," Judy said as she stood up. She hesitated and looked intently at Liz. "Okay, spill it. You've got that funny look on your face again. Hearing voices?"

"As a matter of fact, I am."

"And what did the voice say this time, if I might ask?" Judy asked.

"You might. The voice had a pretty good thought. It said that maybe somebody wanted Nicole to get fat, so she wouldn't be a threat to anyone. The voice said we might look to see who would want her to be fat."

"My take on that would be to see if she was seriously dating anyone." Judy said. "If she was, perhaps the murderer was someone that her male friend or friends were seeing before they started seeing Nicole, and they'd hope that if Nicole got fat, the man who was seeing her would lose interest." She shrugged. "It makes sense to me, but I've started hearing a little voice that tells me I need to get my body in bed. Today has been a little more exciting than I'm used to, and I'm tired. I'll call Maddie and the cooking school and tell you in the morning what I've found out. I also need to call my manager at the hotel and tell her I'm going to be gone a little longer than expected."

CHAPTER FOUR

Liz made a pot of coffee early the next morning and looked over the menu of the cooking school she'd be attending in New Orleans. This was a first for her – going away to a cooking school. She'd easily justified the expense to Roger because not only was the Red Cedar Lodge and Spa booked for months in advance, but her dinners at the lodge were always booked as well. In order to spice things up, she planned on using what she learned in New Orleans for the dinners she served at the lodge, to spice things up a little.

Just reading the cooking school's brochure made her hungry. *If I don't gain weight from pecan praline bites, catfish couvillion, jazzmen rice, Cajun gumbo, and cornbread dressing cake, it will be a miracle. Maybe if I started smoking again and kept it to only two cigarettes a day I wouldn't get fat, but I definitely can't let Roger know, and I'll have to swear Judy to secrecy. When I get back, I could concentrate on giving them up for good, but I'm sure a couple a day while I'm in New Orleans couldn't hurt.*

She could hardly believe what had just crossed her mind, and a moment later, she thought *Where did that come from? I haven't had a cigarette in over twenty years, and I have no intention of starting again. It was hard enough to stop all those years ago. No, that's definitely a road I don't want to go down again.*

She looked at the brochure again. *The rooms in the antebellum mansion where I'll be staying look fabulous! There's so much to do today to get ready, plus*

I may be having lunch at Gertie's if Judy can get in touch with that woman at Nicole's bank.

Liz watered the plants, had a meeting with Bertha, her manager, and checked with her to make sure she and her husband were planning on taking care of her two dogs, Winston and Brandy Boy. Liz got her suitcase out of the garage and began to take clothes out of her dresser and closet. Comfortable clothes, something she could wear when she was cooking.

While she was deciding what to take she heard Judy's voice. "There you are, you big beautiful boy. Winston, one of these days I'm going to kidnap you and take you home with me to Calistoga. I could sure use a good guard like you."

She walked over to the stairs and said, "Liz? Are you down there?"

Liz walked upstairs from the downstairs large apartment where she and Roger lived and said, "Well, is it a go? Are you coming with me?"

"Yep. You're stuck with me. The cooking school said they'd love to have me. I paid with my Visa card, so I'm perfectly legal. I decided they didn't need to know that I don't like to cook, but if I'm asked, I can always say that I'm there to get ideas for the cook I employ at my hotel and spa. That should satisfy them. I rather doubt they'll feel like giving me a refund even if they do find out. And I'd be happy just to be a taster."

Liz laughed softly. "I'm so glad. This is going to be fun, well, as fun as it can be when we're also investigating a voodoo murder. Were you able to get in touch with Maddie?"

"That I was, and we're meeting her at Gertie's Diner at noon. That doesn't give us much time. I need to go back to my cottage and make some calls. I'll be back up here about 11:45, and then we can head over to lunch. Okay with you?"

"Yes, I'm just taking care of a few last-minute things. Do you need to borrow any clothes from me or did you bring enough that you'll be okay?"

"No to both questions. Other than the clothes I've worn to dinner here at the lodge, I just brought clothes for working out and the spa. It's a huge sacrifice on my part, but I guess I'll just have to buy some new clothes in New Orleans." Judy grinned as she walked out the door with a backward wave.

Promptly at 11:45 Judy returned to where Liz was standing in the hallway, saying goodbye to her dogs.

"Well," Judy said, "if it wasn't for Nicole's murder and this voodoo thing, I'd be ecstatic about going to New Orleans. I told you I went there when I was a kid, but I sure wasn't able to take advantage of everything New Orleans has to offer. Are we renting a car?"

"No," Liz said as she ran her hand over Winston's fur coat. "The cooking school van will meet us at the airport and take us to the school. It's in the French Quarter, and I thought we could pretty much walk wherever we wanted to go from there. Plus, from what I read, parking is a nightmare, and honestly, I just didn't want the hassle."

"Sounds good to me. Let's go see Gertie." Judy held the door open and rubbed her stomach with her other hand. "Love seeing you, Liz, but I have to tell you that the highlight of anybody's trip to Red Cedar is a hamburger and milkshake at Gertie's Diner."

While they were driving to Gertie's, Liz's Bluetooth rang in the car and it was Roger, checking in with her before she headed off to New Orleans. They talked about what each of them had been doing, and then Liz told him about Nicole and how Judy was going to join her in New Orleans.

Roger's comment was thoroughly predictable. "Liz, please don't get involved in this." His voice was heavy. "For better or worse, and

I know it's probably for worse, Seth is the police chief in Red Cedar. Let him do his job and stay out of it. You can't take Winston with you, and you'd probably have trouble taking a gun with you. Just leave the whole thing alone."

"Roger, I'm not at all involved," Liz replied, with a light and breezy tone to her voice. "The only thing I intend to do is find out what's up with the voodoo dolls. Since I'm going to be in a place known for voodoo, don't think that will be a problem, plus I'm interested in the subject. Just satisfying my own curiosity."

"Uh, huh," Roger said. "I can tell from your voice that you're probably not telling me something. I'm just glad Judy will be with you. Hopefully, she'll be a steadying influence on you, although knowing her, that seems a stretch."

Liz glanced over at Judy, who was stifling a giggle.

"Anyway, call me when you get there and fill me in on New Orleans," Roger continued. "I've never been there, but I'm sure you'll enjoy it as well as the cooking school. At least, from everything I've heard, I won't have to worry about you eating well."

"I promise I'll be thinking about you as I devour what New Orleans has to offer. Right now, Judy and I are off to see your favorite diner owner, Gertie, for one of her famous hamburgers and milkshakes."

At the mention of Gertie, Roger's tone lightened. "Tell her I said hi. I've got to go. My client just walked through the door. Be safe, and I'll talk to you soon."

"That was good timing. You didn't even have to explain that the reason we're going to Gertie's is to meet someone in connection with Nicole's murder," Judy said when the call had ended.

Liz nodded. "Thank heavens for that. I really don't like to lie to Roger, but sometimes it's better if he doesn't know exactly what I'm doing when it comes to solving murders, or at least attempting to."

"Maybe that's why none of my marriages ever worked out. I had no problem lying to any of them," Judy said with a twinkle in her eye and a sly smile on her face, just as a call came through on her cell phone.

CHAPTER FIVE

"Judging from the lack of parking spaces," Liz said as she pulled her minivan into a space two blocks from the diner, "I think it's safe to assume that Gertie's is packed. I hope she can find somewhere for us to sit."

Judy ended the call to her hotel manager and turned to Liz. "Since she thinks of you as her younger sister and Roger is her tenant, somehow I don't think that's going to be a problem." A few minutes later when she opened the door to the diner and saw the crowd of people waiting to eat, she turned to Liz and groaned. "I may have misspoken. It might be a problem."

Fortunately, she was wrong. As soon as they entered the diner, the indefatigable octogenarian, Gertie, tottered over to them in her stiletto high heels, pencil behind her ear, blond beehive hairdo plastered in place with so much hairspray nothing moved, and chewing a wad of gum. Lately she'd started wearing a big bow at the top of the beehive. Today was a salute to red, in the brightest hue conceivable. She gave both Liz and Judy a hug. "Judy, didn't know ya' was in town. If I had, woulda' had a burger and shake waitin' fer ya'." She gave them both a wink, her wrinkled eyelids shimmering with bronze eyeshadow.

"Gertie," Liz said, "I know you don't take reservations, but you might want to start. From the looks of the crowd in here, it's almost like you're giving away food. How long is the wait going to be? We're meeting someone for lunch."

"Already taken care of. She's in that booth at the back, and don't it beat all, but I was jes' told that Gertie's Diner is now a stop fer some fancy-schmancy bus limo excursion trip." Gertie grinned, revealing several gaps in her smile where her teeth were missing. "They take people from San Francisco to some of them state parks in the northern part of California. Kinda' cool, don'tcha think? I'm gonna' get 'em comin' and goin'. This keeps up, might have to expand this ol' diner. Follow me, ladies."

Gertie was an institution in the city of Red Cedar. She knew everyone and everybody knew her. There wasn't much that happened in the small town that she didn't know about. And if she didn't know about it, she always knew someone who did.

She looked over her shoulder at Liz as they made their way through the crowded diner. "So, ya' gonna' talk to Maddie and see if she knows anything about that voodoo murder, right?"

"Gertie, how do you know about the voodoo dolls?" Liz asked in amazement.

For an answer, Gertie simply rolled her eyes. "Liz, girl, yer' talkin' to Gertie. People tell me everythin'. Might wanna talk to Madame Dika. Remember she's that tarot card reader. Hear she's gettin' active again, and not necessarily in a good way."

She was referring to the murder of Seth's deputy, Leroy, and how Seth visited the tarot card reader and had used that as an alibi, although Madame Dika had not supported it. Liz had heard she'd moved away from Red Cedar after the murder had been solved, and her brother was implicated, but according to Gertie, she was back in the area again.

A moment later, Gertie stopped at a booth at the back of the diner and made the introductions. "Don't know if ya' all have met, but Maddie - this is Liz and Judy. Trust me, they're good people.

Hope ya' all can figure out who offed Nicole. Murder in small towns ain't good fer business." She stepped aside as Liz and Judy sat down in the booth opposite Maddie. "Back with yer' orders in a few minutes. Not botherin' to give you a menu, 'cuz I know what you all want."

And with that she tottered back to the front of the restaurant, ignoring the looks from the people who had just gotten off the tour bus, obviously amazed that this old dynamo with the red bow on her head was the force behind a place to eat that was popular enough that tour companies brought their charges to eat there.

*****

"Maddie, thanks for meeting with us, and I'm glad you know Gertie, because with the tour bus people, I don't think there's any way we would have been able to get a table," Liz said to the attractive green-eyed redhead facing her.

"Gertie is one of my favorite people, and I wouldn't miss a chance to eat here for anything, particularly when Judy told me she was buying," Maddie said with a laugh. "Actually, I'm glad you called. I feel so bad about Nicole. I'm the assistant manager at the bank, and I was devastated when I got a call from the chief of police last night. The staff meeting was pretty rough this morning. Nicole was really liked, and she did a superb job as manager. I have no idea what will happen now." She stopped speaking and brushed away a teardrop from the corner of her eye.

"I never met her," Liz said, "but Judy says she was a wonderful person. The reason we wanted to meet with you is to see if you can shed any light on why someone would have murdered her. I understand there was an incident when she took over the branch where she had to fire someone. Can you tell us about that?"

"Yes. The name of the woman who was fired is Susie LaMotta. I can certainly understand why Nicole fired her. It was long overdue; however, Susie really is a nice person. After she left the bank, she and I continued to correspond by email. She went to Colorado, met a man, and is planning on marrying him soon. She loves her job. Nicole wrote her a letter of recommendation, so I'm certain she wouldn't have had anything to do with Nicole's murder. If you're thinking about going down that road, it's probably a dead end. Thanks to Nicole, Susie got her happy ever after."

"Based on what you're telling me, I would agree," Liz said. Their conversation was interrupted by the arrival of their hamburgers and milkshakes. Each of them was quiet for several minutes as they enjoyed their meal.

Liz paused from eating her hamburger and took a sip of her chocolate milkshake, topped off with a dollop of cream and a cherry on top. "Maddie, I understand Nicole had lost a lot of weight recently. I have a couple of thoughts about that. One, I understand she had a sister she wasn't close to who took the name of Marie Laveau, who is considered to be a voodoo queen in New Orleans."

Maddie looked at her before answering. "Liz, I'm a little unclear as to why you're spending time looking into her murder. You haven't been hired by anyone to help find the murderer, have you?"

Liz was quiet for a moment, trying to decide how to answer the question, which was a valid and fair one. She could also sense Judy looking at her with a quizzical look and probably wondering what she was going to say.

"No, Maddie, I'm not a licensed private investigator, but perhaps you might think of me as an interested person who wants to help a friend. How about calling me an unofficial private investigator? Quite properly, the investigations into Nicole's murder falls under the jurisdiction of the chief of police, the man you spoke with last night. Just between us, I have had a number of dealings with him, and several times I have had to help him with his investigations, because, and I'm not sure how to be politically correct when I say this, some people in Red Cedar consider him to be a rather inept chief of police."

"You can say that again," Maddie said heatedly. "I was furious when I got off the phone with him last night. Talk about insensitive. The man said he really couldn't talk for long because he was filling out some papers about speeding tickets. I couldn't figure out what that had to do with a murder, and whatever it was, it seemed to me it wouldn't be as important as finding out who killed Nicole."

"That's why I'm involved," Liz said. "I didn't personally know Nicole, but my friend Judy did. Unfortunately, we were the ones who discovered her body. I sensed she didn't have a lot of people in her corner, and since I've been fairly successful in helping solve other cases like this one, I find that I simply can't walk away from it with a clear conscience."

"I'm glad," Maddie said, dipping a long, thick French fry into the pool of ketchup on the white greaseproof paper lining the red plastic dinner basket her meal was served in. "Nicole deserves to have someone help her. It really seems like a sick twist of fate that once she'd finally gotten her life together, she was murdered."

"There's another reason I'm involved. I'm leaving tomorrow morning for New Orleans, which has a reputation for being pretty much the home of voodoo and things of that nature. I don't know if you're aware of it, but someone had been sending voodoo dolls to Nicole. As a matter of fact, there was one lying on the porch next to where we found her. I thought I might do a little research while I'm in New Orleans and see what I can find out.

"I think there must be some sort of connection between the voodoo dolls and Nicole's murder. What better place is there to look for that connection than in New Orleans?"

CHAPTER SIX

While Liz had been talking, Maddie had finished her hamburger and had pushed her basket away from her. "Liz, Judy, I'll tell you what I know. Nicole told me once that she and her sister were estranged, and that they were as different as night and day. She said her sister was really into voodoo, thus the name change. Since voodoo dolls were involved, perhaps she had something to do with it."

"I heard that she changed her name to Marie Leveau. That certainly is a strange thing to do, and with the voodoo dolls Nicole had received, I would think she would have to be a person of interest," Judy said, "although that would seem almost too coincidental."

"Yes, if you ask me, it does seem pretty convenient, but then again, you just never know what happens in families. Since they hadn't had much of a relationship, why would her sister do something like that now?" Maddie picked up her milkshake and drank the rest of it through the straw. There was a loud noise when she reached the bottom of the tall glass.

"My thoughts exactly," Liz said. "However, my husband spent many years as a criminal defense attorney, and if he was here I'm sure he would say that there is always the possibility that's what Nicole's sister would want you to think, that it was too convenient, and so you'd dismiss her."

"I hadn't thought of that," Maddie said. "I suppose in some convoluted way, in makes sense. Liz, a few minutes ago you said the word one, when you asked about her sister. Is there a two?"

"Yes, I was wondering if she was seeing anyone, say a male friend? Would you happen to know anything about her social life?"

"Yes, she was seeing a man named Cody Evans. She started seeing him a couple of months ago. She laughed when she told me how they'd met. Nicole loved dogs and had taken her standard poodle, Saint, named for the New Orleans Saints, to a dog park near her home. She said that her dog had gone over to a man and literally pushed the man over to where Nicole was standing. She told me it was like Saint knew she and the man were meant for each other."

"You're kidding. That would be something to see," Liz said laughing.

"Nicole and Cody got to talking after it happened, one thing led to another, and soon they were meeting at the dog park regularly. Coffees were next, and then dinner dates. Although she never said so, I had the impression they were getting very serious. She had a photograph of him on a cabinet in her office. I hadn't even thought about him until now. I wonder if he knows."

"I have no idea," Liz said. "I'd call him, but it would seem pretty strange getting a call from me, a total stranger. I hate to ask you to do this, but if you could call him, and use the pretext that Nicole had often spoken of him, you could find out if he knows about her death. What concerns me is that I'm sure Seth wouldn't think to find out if she was seeing anyone."

"Don't you think Cody would have heard about it from someone or the media?" Maddie asked.

"He might have, and you could use that as the reason for your call. Tell him you were sure he'd heard and just wanted to tell him how sorry you are, because you knew he was important to Nicole."

"Yes, I can do that. Nicole mentioned once that he was a stockbroker, one of the few in Red Cedar, so it shouldn't be too hard to find him."

"Maddie, I have another favor to ask," Liz said.

"What's that?"

"I'd like you to tell me how he sounds when you speak with him."

"What do you mean, how he sounds?"

"Well, I guess what I'm asking you to do is find out if he sounds sincerely devastated or phony devastated. Could you also ask him if he has any idea who would have a reason or want to kill Nicole? When you're finished, mention that a private investigator got in touch with you at the bank this morning, and tell him that she would like to talk to him. Say that you just wanted him to be aware a woman by the name of Liz Lucas would be calling him. I'll need you to give me his phone number. I'm leaving town in the morning, so I'll have to call him late this afternoon. Can you do all that for me?" Liz asked.

Maddie was quiet for several moments, then she said, "Yes, I can do that. It's the least I can do if it helps find whoever killed Nicole. Why don't you give me your phone number, and I'll call you as soon as I talk to Cody?" She looked at Liz and Judy in turn. "I have to tell you that I'm dreading the call. I've never done anything like this before."

"Think of it as doing something for Nicole," Liz said earnestly. "If she cared about Cody as much as you think she did, I'm sure she would appreciate your calling him. I'd do it, but since I don't know him, I think an introduction by you would be helpful. Thanks for agreeing to do this."

She was interrupted by the appearance of Gertie at their table. "Well, ladies, how were the eats? Good as usual?"

Gertie cocked her head in Liz's direction. "Move over." She sat down next to Liz and said, "When ya' goin' to New Orleans?"

"How did you know I was going?" Liz asked.

"Sweetheart, tol' ya' before. Not much I don't know about the goins' on in this town. While yer' down there see if ya' can get some info on those voodoo dolls. Had a woman in here a coupla' days ago, and she had one of 'em layin' on the table here. Gotta' tell ya', it gave me the creeps. Really a weird lookin' thing. Like to hear what ya' find out."

"Gertie," Liz asked, "did you know the woman who had the doll?"

"Naw, can't say as I did. Ain't never seen her before. Pretty lookin' thing though."

"Gertie, this could be important. When was she in here?"

Gertie put her elbows on the table, interlaced her hands, and put her chin on them. "Give me a minute. Need to have me a think 'bout it." She was quiet for several long moments, obviously searching her memory. "Okay, I got it now. Was yesterday. Got so many people in here lately with all these bus people, hard to remember, but I'm sure of it."

She nodded and smiled, looking pleased with herself. "I remember 'cuz I was thinkin' it was lucky she got a table 'cuz a coupla' minutes later a big bus full of people came in, hungry as could be. All of 'em had heard 'bout my hamburgers and milkshakes. Darn near ran outta' food. Gonna' have to start buyin' more of the makins' for burgers, tell ya' that."

"Gertie, what did she look like? I don't know why, but I think it may be important."

"Girl, yer' gonna' love me, altho' I know ya' already do. I can do ya' one better than a description. Jes' 'membered I took a photo of all them bus people sittin' in their booths, and realized I'd gotten a pic of that woman, too. Didn't have the right angle on the camera, so I took another one. Thought I might use it fer advertisin', not that I need to advertise, the way this place has become gangbusters. I'm purty sure I got a good pic of her. I'll get my camera. Back in a sec."

They watched as the octogenarian institution toddled off to the hostess stand which had several drawers in it. She reached into one and pulled her cell phone from it. A moment later she sat back down in their booth.

"Might take me a coupla' minutes to find it," she said as she scrolled through her photos. "Been takin' a lot of 'em lately. Ain't sure what I'm gonna' do with 'em, but if I ever do decide to expand this joint, might wanna' show 'em to a banker or money man. Actually, Liz, jes' might talk to Roger. Way he's got clients comin' and goin' all day, figured he's probably rich as Midas 'bout now."

"Don't think so," Liz said with a laugh. "Or if he is, I don't know about it."

"Yep, here 'tis. Knew I probably had one of her. She was sittin' in that booth over there," Gertie said, pointing her finger towards a booth and putting her phone on the table, so the three of them could look at the image on the screen. "Tol' ya' she was a looker."

On the screen of Gertie's cell phone was the picture of a very attractive woman. The woman had long blond hair pulled back from her face with a barrette clasp. Her complexion was flawless, and her eyes were a deep blue. She wore little makeup and had on a blue sweater that matched her eyes. Large round diamond studs were prominent on each earlobe.

She appeared to be lost in thought, with a wistful smile on her face. Liz could see why Gertie thought it would make a good photo for an advertisement. She could just imagine the headline above the photo would run something like, "Gertie's Diner – Good For The Stomach, Good For The Soul."

Gertie had been standing several feet away from the table when she took the photograph, and the photo clearly showed a voodoo doll lying on the table in front of the woman. It looked very much like the doll Liz and Judy had found at the scene of the murder. Liz didn't want Gertie and Maddie to know that she had the voodoo doll that had been found next to Nicole's body.

"Gertie, would you mind emailing that photo to me? I have no idea what I'll do with it, but it might come in handy."

"No problem, Doll. I'm sending it right now." She tapped the phone with ease. It was a top-of-the-line model for an old lady, and Liz was impressed by Gertie's technical expertise. "You oughta' have it now. Check yer phone. Hey, while we're at it, lemme' get a pic of the three of you. Good-lookin' as you all are, might use that pic in some advertisin'." Gertie waved her hands around to set the shot up. "Judy, Liz, you get on either side of Maddie. Yeah, that's good. Say cheese," she said as she snapped the photo.

"Gertie, send that one to me, too, if you would. I'm not advertising anything, but I don't have too many photos with Judy and me in them."

When Gertie was finished Liz took her phone out of her purse and saw that both photos had been sent to her. "Thanks, Gertie. When I'm down in New Orleans, I'll see if I can find out anything about the voodoo doll in this photo."

"Well, have a good time for me, and eat a coupla' of them pralines fer ol' Gertie. Ain't never been there, but it's one of them things I wanna' do before the bucket gets me. Ya' know what I mean?"

"I do, but I think you mean it's on your bucket list."

"Yeah, whatever. Have a good time and tell that handsome hunk of yers' I said hi. Speakin' of which, when's he gonna' be back from the city?" Gertie looked around the dining room, making sure everything was under control, before turning her attention back to Liz.

"He'll be back in a couple of days, and become your best customer once again," Liz said with a laugh. Roger rented his business office from Gertie, and it was conveniently located next to Gertie's Diner.

When she was gone, Liz turned back to Maddie and said, "Thanks again for taking the time to meet with me. I'll look forward to your call later today." She turned to Judy and said, "Understand you're treating for lunch, thanks." Judy took several bills out of her purse and put them on the check Gertie had left on the table.

Maddie glanced at them and said, "Thanks for paying for my lunch, Judy, but at least let me add a little to the tip." She opened her purse, and as she did so, a tape recorder fell out of it.

"Recording our conversation?" Liz asked in a teasing voice, only half-joking.

"No, I read something recently about how if you wrote down or dictated the events of the day, you became much more organized. I think it works. I've been dictating pretty much everything I've done for the last couple of months, and I'm finding I'm not only more organized, I really am getting a lot more ticked off my to-do list."

"Good for you. We can all use a little help in that area. Anyway, put your money away. Judy left more than enough money on the table including a generous tip for Gertie," Liz said as the three of them stood up and left the booth. Moments later one of the young busboys had cleaned the table, eager bus tour people had been seated, and were primed and ready to order the diner specialty – Gertie's Famous Hamburger and Chocolate Milkshake.

On their way back to the lodge, Judy asked, "What did you think of Maddie?"

"About what I expected. Didn't seem like she was too close to Nicole, but she knew things about her which I'd expect. Why do you ask?"

"I think you missed it," Judy said, "but I would swear when Gertie said she'd like to take a picture of the three of us, Maddie didn't want to, but didn't know how to get out of it."

Liz thought nothing of it. "I didn't have that sense, Judy. I think your imagination may have been in overdrive. I do have a favor to ask of you, though."

"Sure, what is it?"

"I'd like to take a little drive out to Madame Dika's. She's into tarot cards and things like that. Maybe she knows something about voodoo dolls."

"At this point, I'm just along for the ride. She sounds interesting."

"She is, but keep your purse next to you, and don't listen to her when she says she can tell things about you by feeling your jewelry when its in her hands," Liz said, hurrying towards the car.

"Do I sense there's a bit of a dishonest nature in Madame Dika?"

"That might be the understatement of the year. It won't take long."

CHAPTER SEVEN

Liz pulled over to the curb on the street in front of the Madame Dika's purple house and turned the engine off. When she saw the parked car in the driveway, she assumed Madame Dika was conducting a tarot card reading.

Judy had also noticed it and said, "Looks like she has a client. Should we come back?"

"No. She usually leaves a note on the door that says to come in, and she'll be with you when her reading is completed."

Just as Liz expected, they found the note on the front door, entered the house, and settled down to wait for the session to be over. After a few minutes, Judy got up and walked over to the bookcases that lined the walls, looking at the different books that dealt with all kinds of extra sensory perception. Madame Dika's library spanned the whole genre, with everything from angels to love potion spells.

Judy looked at Liz and raised her eyebrows. "Interesting," she said.

A few moments later the door to Madame Dika's tarot card reading room opened and Seth Williams, the chief of police, walked out. He did a double take when he recognized Liz and Judy. All Liz could think about was how involved he'd been in Madame Dika's readings when his deputy, Leroy, had been murdered.

"Liz, surprised to see ya' here. Didn't think ya' believed in this stuff," Seth said nervously.

Liz's greeting was cool. "I might say the same, Seth. I thought you'd gotten your fill of tarot card readings after Leroy's murder," she responded.

"Well, that was then, and this is now. Madame Dika always knows what's in the cards for me," he said laughing, shuffling his feet. "Get it? What's in the cards? Anyway, I wanted to find out how that raise for me was lookin'. She said she's pretty sure I'm gonna' get it."

"Well, I suppose in that case, congratulations are in order. Congratulations."

Just then Madame Dika walked into the room and saw Liz. Her expression was not one of welcome. Seth looked at both women and must have decided it was time for him to leave. "Better get back to the station. Got a lotta' work I gotta' get done if I'm gonna' get that raise. Nice seein' you ladies," he said with a fake smile on his face as he walked out the door.

Madame Dika addressed Liz with distaste. "Ms. Lucas, what are you doing here? Don't you think you've done enough to upset my life? You were responsible for ruining it, and the reason I had to leave town. I'm starting over, but I don't want anything to do with you." Madame Dika crossed her arms over her ample chest, her jet-black hair falling to her shoulders from beneath the red scarf she wore in a turban style.

Liz stood up. "I won't keep you long, Madame Dika. I'd just like to know if you have any knowledge of voodoo. Do you?"

"And what if I did? Why would I tell you? I don't owe you anything after everything you've done to me." Madame Dika took a step backwards.

"That's true, but since you're outside the city limits of Red Cedar, I believe you're doing business under the jurisdiction of the county. I know the sheriff well. Might be interesting to give him a call and see if you have all the necessary permits you're supposed to have. If your business was closed down, that fresh start might be a little difficult for you."

Madame Dika's eyes flashed with hatred as she regarded Liz. "I know many things about all sorts of strange and occult things. Voodoo is very popular in the New Orleans area, in Louisiana. They use spells for good and bad things. They also make dolls they call voodoo dolls, as well as something called gris-gris. That's when physical things are used, like a strand of hair or a cutting from a fingernail or toenail. It can be for evil or to bring luck. The gris-gris is usually put in a pouch, and the person has to keep it on their body for it to work."

"Can voodoo be used to kill someone?" Judy asked.

"I don't know. I don't practice it," Madame Dika said. She shifted her gaze so she could look out the window. Another car had pulled up outside. The sound of a car door being shut was followed by approaching footsteps. "I see that my next appointment is here. You'll have to leave," she said, walking over to the door and holding it open while she smiled at her client who was entering the room.

"Thank you, Madame Dika," Liz said as she and Judy walked out the door.

Madame Dika ignored her as she ushered her client into her house.

"She's a real piece of work. Is she always that friendly?" Judy asked sarcastically after they'd gotten back in Liz's minivan.

"To me, yes. When I first had a reading from her, she was all smiles and charm. Once she discovered I was there to see what I could find out about Leroy's murder, our relationship went down a steep hill."

"Was she any good? Did she give you a reading?"

"She did. I think people who go to her are desperate and will probably believe anything she says. I definitely didn't have the feeling I was in the presence of an enlightened person or someone who could tell me anything about my life that I didn't already know."

"I haven't thought of this in several years, but when my daughter, Tiffany, turned twenty-one, I took her to the Biltmore Hotel in Santa Barbara," Judy said. "She went to the university there and was always talking about how fancy the hotel was and that someday she'd like to stay there."

"That's a pretty nice birthday present, Judy. The Biltmore is not known as a place to go if you're trying to save money."

"I know, but what the heck? You only turn twenty-one once. Anyway, we walked out on the pier and there was a fortune teller near the end of it. I thought it would be fun on Tiffany's birthday for her to have her fortune told. She agreed, but only if I would have mine done as well."

"And I'm assuming you did."

"I did, and it was the biggest waste of twenty dollars I've ever spent. The fortune teller took my hand and told me that I didn't do any kind of manual labor."

"Well, you don't," Liz said, reversing the minivan onto the pavement.

"No, but she was supposed to have this gift, and anyone could tell from holding my hand that I don't do manual labor." Judy held her hands out and wriggled her fingers. "Come on. I've got acrylic nails, a French manicure, and a couple of large diamond rings. You don't need ESP to immediately know that about me. Like yours, it went downhill from there."

"What about Tiffany? Did she receive any words of wisdom from the fortune teller?"

"Oh yeah. The fortune teller told her she would fall in love with a handsome stranger and have a good life. That was about the total sum of our experience. What a rip-off. I still get mad when I think about it."

"I can see why. I felt the same way about Madame Dika, although Seth obviously still believes in her."

"Somehow, that doesn't surprise me," Judy said with an exaggerated sigh. "No, not in the least."

CHAPTER EIGHT

Liz spent the rest of the day getting ready for her trip to New Orleans. Judy had been able to reschedule the spa treatments she'd planned for the following day for that afternoon. Liz was going to drive her minivan to the airport and park it in the long-term lot. Their flight left at 9:00 a.m., so they decided to leave Red Cedar Lodge at 5:30 a.m. Traffic getting to the San Francisco airport could be brutal on a weekday morning at that time, and they didn't want to miss their flight.

When Liz finished packing, she lifted her suitcase off of the bed, and put it on the floor for any last-minute packing she'd need to do in the morning. She carefully took the voodoo doll that Seth had given her, as well as the two Judy had given her, out of her purse and put them in her suitcase.

I hope I can find something out about these things. Surely, in a city that's known for black magic and things like that, there must be someone who can tell me about them. And I still don't understand why someone would want to kill Nicole. It just doesn't make any sense to me.

She was looking in her closet to see if she'd missed packing something she'd regret not taking when her cell phone rang. "This is Liz," she said, noticing that no name had come up on the cell phone's screen.

"Hi, Liz, it's Maddie. I just got off the phone with Cody." Liz could hear Maddie swallow. "Oh, Liz, it was so sad. A friend of his has a son who does some intern work in the coroner's office, and he'd met Nicole when Cody had brought her over to the house to meet his father and mother. He just happened to be there to pick up something. Anyway, he had his father call and break the news to Cody. He sounded heartbroken, legitimately. I feel so sorry for him. He told me they were planning on getting married."

"When a murder has been committed," Liz said, "I'm told the textbook standard is to look at the people who are emotionally close to the victim, but from what you're telling me, it sounds like he didn't have anything to do with the murder."

"I know nothing about all of this," Maddie said. "As a matter of fact, Nicole is the first person I've ever known who was murdered. I just feel for Cody. Anyway, I told him about you, and he's expecting your call. He did tell me he had no idea who would do something like this."

"You did a very good job, Maddie, thank you. He probably doesn't know anything, but I'd like to talk to him anyway, particularly since I didn't know Nicole. I'll give him a call in a few minutes."

"Well, thanks again for lunch. I don't think there's anything else I can do for you or for poor Nicole, but if something comes up, would it be okay if I called you? Maybe I'll hear something at work."

"Yes, please feel free to call anytime if you hear anything. Even if it doesn't mean anything to you, it might be the link we need to help solve her murder. Again, thanks for taking the time to have lunch with us."

"Enjoy New Orleans, and I hope you find out something that will help Nicole, although I guess nothing can change her fate now."

"Again, many thanks for your help. I need to call Cody and take care of a few more things that need to be done around here."

*****

A few minutes later, Liz heard a man answer her call and say, "Hello, this is Cody Evans."

"Mr. Evans, my name is Liz Lucas. I believe Maddie Sanders mentioned that I would be calling you regarding Nicole Rogers. I understand you had a relationship with her, and I want to tell you how sorry I am for your loss."

Even though it was quiet on the other end of the phone, Liz was pretty sure Cody was crying softly. She thought he might have placed his hand over his phone to mask the sound.

Liz felt like she was intruding on his grief. "I won't keep you long, Mr. Evans, but I would like to ask you a couple of questions. Would that be all right?"

He let out a deep sigh and replied in a shaky voice. "Yes, if it would help find out who did this horrible thing, I'm happy to help, but I don't think I know anything."

"First of all, I understand that Nicole had a sister. Did she ever mention her?"

"Yes, she often talked about how she really had no family other than a sister who she hadn't spoken to in years."

"She actually told you she hadn't spoken to her in years, is that correct?"

"Yes," Cody said. "I'm really certain about it because we were having dinner in San Francisco. I'd taken her down there because she always told me how she loved Creole food, but Red Cedar was too small to support a Creole restaurant. While we were eating at one that I'd found on the internet, she told me about how her sister had gone over to what she called 'the dark side' several years ago, and she hadn't spoken to her since that happened. She told me her sister had legally changed her name to Marie Leveau, because she'd become a voodoo practitioner."

"Do you know if Nicole was involved in the practice of voodoo?"

"Definitely not." Cody said emphatically. "She told me that she grew up in a poor parish outside of New Orleans where the practice of voodoo was pretty common. She said it might appeal to some people, but she thought it was pretty much a lot of hocus pocus, or words to that effect."

Liz knew what Nicole meant. She'd always thought the same thing herself, although recent events were beginning to make her question if maybe there wasn't something to it. "Did she ever mention she was having problems with people at the bank where she was the manager?"

"One time we were talking about people we worked with, and she mentioned that she had to fire an employee when she first took over as manager. She said the woman was really angry at first, but it had a silver lining, because the woman moved to Colorado, met the man of her dreams, and was even able to get a good job because of Nicole's recommendation."

"I hate to ask you this Mr. Evans, but do you have any enemies who would want to hurt you by murdering a woman you were seeing?"

"Liz, please call me Cody, and I was more than seeing Nicole. Last week I asked her to marry me, and she agreed. We were planning on getting married next spring. As far as someone who would want to hurt me through Nicole, I have no idea. I can't think of anyone who would hate me enough to do that."

"What about relationships with other women? When you became involved with Nicole, did you break off any relationships? Were you involved with someone prior to her?"

He was quiet for several long moments, and then cleared his throat. "Yes, I was dating a woman, but we weren't exclusive. She wasn't very happy when I told her I was ending our relationship because I was seeing another woman, and that relationship was getting serious. Actually, she was furious, but I think it was just a momentary thing. I haven't spoken to her since."

"Does she live in Red Cedar?" Liz asked.

"No, she lives in Bodega Bay. We met about a year ago when she inherited some money when her father died. She was looking for an investment adviser, and I was recommended to her. One thing led to another and we started seeing each other."

"What can you tell me about her?"

"Well, she owns an insurance agency which she inherited from her father. I guess she started working there when she was in high school, so it was a pretty natural career for her."

"What's her name, and what does she look like?"

"Her name is Candace Norgan. She has long blond hair, a nice complexion, and dark blue eyes. I suppose a lot of people would find her attractive. I did once."

Liz immediately thought of the woman in Gertie's photograph taken in the diner. The one with the voodoo doll on the table.

"Did Candace know Nicole's name?" Liz asked.

Cody was quiet, then he said, "I don't know if I told her Nicole's name, but I do remember telling her that Nicole was the manager of a bank in Red Cedar. I suppose she could have found out, since there are only three banks in town. Why? Do you think she might have had something to do with the murder?"

"I have no idea, but I'm trying to look under every rock. Cody, I'm leaving for New Orleans in the morning, and I need to do a few more things before I go. Let me give you my cell number, and if you think of something, please call me."

"All right. I hope you find out who did this horrible thing," he said with a catch in his voice.

"Cody, I promise you, I'll do my best."

CHAPTER NINE

After Liz ended the call with Cody, the little voice in her head started in. "*Don't get involved in this. There are darker things in this world than you know about, and this is way out of your comfort zone,*" the voice said.

Well, it's too late now, Liz thought to herself. *I'm committed, plus Cody sounds like he's a very nice person. Maybe I can help.*

"*No, Liz, not without hurting yourself,*" the voice said. "*Walk away from this.*"

Liz shook her head and was thinking about what the voice had said when her cell phone rang. She noticed Cody's name flash up on her screen and said, "Hi, Cody. Did you remember something?"

"After you called I was trying to remember if there was a link between Candace and Nicole."

"Since you called, I'm assuming that you found one," she said evenly.

"Well, I have no idea if it's important, relevant, or even worth mentioning, but I decided to let you be the judge of that. Here's what I remembered. On the day I told Candace I was going to break up with her, I went to her office to tell her I no longer wanted to see her, that I had found someone else. I didn't think it would be right to do it over the phone."

"That was a very thoughtful thing to do."

"Yeah, well who knows? Anyway, I walked into her office, and she was sitting at her desk reading a magazine. I asked her what she was reading, and she said an article about Creole food and the whole New Orleans voodoo thing. I told her that was a coincidence, because I had just been to a Creole restaurant in San Francisco the evening before. We talked about it and then I told her I was sorry, but I no longer wanted to see her. She was furious and asked if I'd taken some good-looking Cajun woman to the Creole restaurant, and if she'd cast some sort of voodoo spell on me."

"That must have been a very difficult conversation, Cody," Liz said.

"Believe me, it was. I told her no, the woman was a manager of a bank. I'd taken the woman there because she was from Louisiana. I still don't remember giving her Nicole's name, but I'm sure she could have easily found that out given that she was the manager of a bank and from Louisiana. I rather doubt that either one of the other two managers of the banks in town are from Louisiana," he said with a bitter laugh. "Anyway, for what it's worth, there it is. I have no idea what you can do with it, if anything, but wanted to let you know."

"Cody, I don't have any idea either, but I'm glad you told me. As I said, you never know what will prove to be important. Did Nicole ever mention anything to you about finding voodoo dolls, like someone had been putting them in different places where that person knew Nicole would find them?"

Liz told him about the doll falling out of Nicole's locker and also about the doll that had the word "Bacalou" written on it and the skull and crossbones. After she told him, he was silent and said, "No, she never mentioned anything to me about that. It sounds like this was well thought out by whoever left the dolls. I just can't imagine who would want to deliver scary voodoo dolls to Nicole."

"Nor do I, Cody, but I plan to look into it while I'm in New Orleans. Again, if you think of anything else, please call me."

"I will, and thanks for trying to find out who murdered Nicole. I know at some point I'll have to grieve for what might have been, but right now I'm beginning to feel angrier than I have ever been in my life, and it's not a feeling I like."

"Cody, there are different steps involved in the grieving process. Don't try to rush it. I know it's a trite saying, but time is a great healer. Give yourself some time."

"Yeah, I've been there and done that. When I was twelve, we were living in San Francisco. My mother was walking out of a drugstore when she got hit by a stray bullet fired by some gangbanger and died."

"Oh, Cody, I am so sorry. This must be like déjà vu for you. No one should have to go through something like that even once, let alone twice."

"I agree. I know time heals, but this one's going to take even longer. When you're twelve you're a little more absorbed by yourself than you are at thirty-one. I just hope I can make it through this, but there are moments I have my doubts."

"Cody, I've got a big shoulder to cry on and I always have an open ear. If you ever feel like talking to someone, please call me. I don't have answers, but I sure can listen."

"Thanks, Liz. You don't even know me, but I appreciate your offer, and I just might take you up on it."

*****

When the last of the guests had left the lodge that evening, and the continental breakfast Bertha would fix in the morning was fully prepped and ready to go, Liz walked downstairs, let Winston out, and got ready for bed.

Her thoughts turned back to Nicole and Cody. Even though she hadn't met him, she liked him through the conversations they had shared by telephone. His grief seemed genuine, and while she knew it would take a long time for the pain of Nicole's death to go away, she hoped she could find the killer and at least have him feel that justice had been served. That, on top of having your mother murdered when you were only twelve, was enough to break anyone.

She wished she could stay in Red Cedar and look for Nicole's killer, but since she really had no personal involvement in the case, other than the fact that she and Judy had been the ones to find Nicole, she couldn't justify staying. She hoped Seth would be able to find the murderer, although given her conversation with him earlier when she'd called to see if he had found out anything, along with seeing him at Madame Dika's, she doubted it.

Seth had told her that as soon as he finished filling out his traffic forms, he'd get to it. She was still amazed that the good citizens of Red Cedar had elected him as their police chief, not just once, but several times.

Knowing it was going to be a short night, after she let Winston in, Liz quickly fell into a deep sleep. The last thought she had before she fell asleep was *I hope I can find something out about voodoo. Surely, in a city that's known for black magic and things like that, there must be someone who can tell me about them. And even more importantly, maybe they can even tell me who killed Nicole.* As she slept through the night, her dreams were populated with voodoo dolls and black magic symbols.

CHAPTER TEN

The next day, the van occupied by Liz and Judy pulled up to the Desiree Richarde antebellum mansion in New Orleans' French Quarter. Liz had read that the house was named for the wife of a well-known Louisiana senator who, prior to the Civil War, had scandalized the society of that time by marrying a Creole woman. The photograph in the brochure had shown a beautiful woman with a pale caramel complexion, jet black hair, and adorned with jewels.

The story in the brochure said the senator had become enamored of her when he'd attended a quadroon ball. White men attended these balls and often became a benefactor for a woman who then became his concubine. He died shortly after marrying her, leaving all of his property to her. She spent the rest of her life helping free people of color, particularly women, and to this day her name invoked awe and devotion for what she had been able to accomplish.

While the driver got their suitcases out of the van, she looked up at the three-story mansion. It epitomized the French Quarter style, brick with green painted shutters, balconies running the length of the mansion on each floor, intricate wrought iron railings overall, and baskets and planters spilling over with flowers. It was one of the most beautiful homes Liz had ever seen. The brochure said that although the home had been modernized, many of the original features remained.

"Liz, this may be the most beautiful place I've ever seen. I can't believe we're actually going to stay here. This may be the best vacation I've ever had." The awe in Judy's voice was reflected in Liz's thoughts.

Liz tipped the driver and pounded the brass door knocker twice. The door was immediately opened by a large black woman wearing a maid's uniform and a white apron.

"Come in, come in, ladies," the maid said with a wide smile. "You two are the last to arrive." She nodded at each of them in turn. "One of you must be Liz Lucas and the other must be Judy Rasmussen. Just follow me, and I'll take you to your room."

Liz and Judy stared at the entryway in front of them which contained a large round mahogany table in the center, on which was a huge vase filled with freshly cut flowers. Old oil portraits hung on the high-ceilinged walls. Reluctantly, they followed the maid up the highly polished wooden stairs, holding on to the ornate wrought iron handrail. Halfway down the hall, the maid opened the door to a large room.

"This is your room. The bedroom is through that door. It's got two queen size beds in it, and the bathroom is next to it. If there's anything I can do for you, please let me know. You can press 1 on the telephone to reach one of the staff. Wine will be served in the main living room at 5:00 this evening, and dinner will follow. That's when you'll be given suggestions about things you can do during the time you'll be staying with us, plus you'll also be told about the cooking school schedule."

As Liz and Judy started to unpack, there was a knock on the door. When Liz opened it, a younger maid was standing there with a plate of cookies and a jug in her hand. "Miss Lawson tol' me to bring you these pralines and southern sweet iced tea." She walked over to the mahogany coffee table and put them on it, beside some glasses which were already there. As she turned to walk back to the door, she saw Liz's open suitcase just inside the bedroom and the three voodoo dolls along with the note with the skull and cross bones on it. Her face blanched, and she stumbled while she quickly tried to leave the room.

"Wait," Liz said, calling her back. "What's wrong? Can you tell me something about these voodoo dolls?"

"Ma'am, what you doin' with them things?" The maid spoke in a whisper. "That's black magic. Who gave you those?"

"It's a long story. What do you know about them?"

"Nothin', Ms. Lucas, nothin'. Don' know nothin' 'bout those things." She turned and hurried out the door.

Liz bit into one of the decadent pralines and took a long drink of iced tea, noticing that Judy was doing the same. Judy looked like she was waiting to see what Liz was going to say about the conversation with the maid.

"Well, that's interesting," Liz said as she turned to face Judy. "We've been here for five minutes, and these voodoo dolls have already scared the help. Swell. She knew a lot more than she was saying, that's for sure."

"I agree," Judy said. "But I have to say, this is getting a bit scary."

"*Liz,*" the little voice in her head said with a tone of urgency, "*Doesn't that tell you something? Leave those things alone. They can only hurt you.*"

CHAPTER ELEVEN

Liz and Judy woke up to the sounds of the French Quarter. Delivery trucks, a clarinet, horns beeping, and Southern accents blended together, creating a true Southern feel. Liz lay in bed, savoring the richness of their surroundings. She thought about the breakfast they'd been told about the night before, looked over at Judy and said, "I'm going to shower and then you're up. After that fabulous dinner last night, I can't wait to see what's being served for breakfast, and I don't want to miss a thing."

"I'll be right behind you," Judy said, sitting up.

The cooking school operated at the Desiree Richarde mansion had a fixed schedule for its students, twelve in total, who were from all over the United States. They were to prepare lunch and do the prep work for dinner from 10:00 to 12:30 for the next four days. Lunch would be served at 1:00 and they were free in the afternoon to explore and experience New Orleans. There were a number of suggested activities and the cooking school provided guides if anyone was interested. Each student was expected to help serve food at either one lunch or one dinner. Other than that, the only thing required was simply to immerse oneself in food. Wine would be served at 5:00 in the evening with dinner following.

Liz and Judy went downstairs to the continental breakfast which Celia Brisson, the head of the cooking school, had promised the night before would be worth getting up for. She hadn't exaggerated. Several small tables had been set up for breakfast in the garden room. A long table had been placed against the back wall with the breakfast offerings displayed on it.

Good grief, last night was incredible, but this is every bit as unbelievable, Liz thought, examining the offerings on the table: fresh fruit; grilled shrimp and cheese grits; poached eggs served on crab cakes; thick ham slices with red-eye gravy; homemade biscuits; onion flatbread; beignets sprinkled with powdered sugar; hot cocoa with whipped cream; and coffee.

Judy looked at Liz and said, "If every meal is like this, we might as well charter a plane to go home 'cuz I sure won't be able to get a commercial seat belt around my waist."

"I was thinking the same thing," Liz said, wondering where to start. She decided on a little bit of everything.

The morning was spent preparing lunch and prepping for dinner. The chef of the day instructed them in the basics of Cajun Creole cooking. Liz had been nervous about attending, worried that the others would be real professional chefs and being self-taught, she'd look foolish next to them. She needn't have worried. There was only one chef in the group. The rest were people who just enjoyed food and cooking. Judy began to look relaxed with the same realization and rolled up her sleeves with the rest of them.

The staples of Southern cooking were well represented as they prepared dirty rice with black beans, catfish, sweet potato bread pudding, braised greens, and pecan praline bites. Liz noticed that a lot of the ingredients of the luncheon dishes were reinvented for dinner. Liz and Judy volunteered to be luncheon servers, wanting to get it out of the way early on. When lunch was over, they walked into the large kitchen with the last plates from the table, glad they'd finished their serving duties for the time they'd be at the school.

Liz looked at Judy and said, "Judy, we might as well go to that museum and get that over with. It's only a couple of blocks from here, then we'll have the other three days to do what we want. Let's go up to our room and change clothes."

The students had been instructed to leave their cell phones in their rooms. The chefs didn't want cell phones interrupting the flow of the food preparation. When Liz and Judy walked into their room, Liz noticed she had a message from Cody. She called him back.

"I'm so glad you called, Liz. I decided to go home during my lunch break, and I found a box wrapped like a present on my front porch. I opened it and Liz, inside was a small cloth pouch. I pulled the drawstring open and there were feathers, wood, ashes, and a bunch of other natural things in it. I've never seen anything like it and given what happened to Nicole, I have to say that I'm spooked. I have no idea why someone would give me such a thing. I'm beginning to wonder if someone wants me dead as well. I know you just got there yesterday, but have you found out anything yet?"

"No, in fact I was on my way to the Voodoo Museum when I noticed that you'd called. I'm going to take the voodoo dolls and the note over there and see if anyone knows anything about them. I'll also tell them about the pouch. I'll call you or text you if I find out anything. I'm sure it's nothing to worry about. Someone is probably just having a lot of fun, unfortunately at your expense. Try and forget about it."

"I sure hope that's all it is. I really don't know how much more I can take right now. I'll wait to hear from you."

Liz told Judy what Cody had said and hoped they could find something out at the museum they were going to.

Judy jumped up. "Let's go. I'm ready. I wouldn't miss this for the world."

CHAPTER TWELVE

Half an hour later, after walking along Dumaine Street, the two of them entered the brightly colored New Orleans Historic Voodoo Museum and paid the $7.00 admission fee. The attendant who collected the fee wore a yellow turban, a bright red blouse, and a long yellow and red skirt. Several bracelets and necklaces adorned her arms and neck. "Feel free to walk around in the display rooms and please, don't miss the gift shop. Let me know if I can help you with anything. Actually, everyone who works here is very knowledgeable about voodoo, so we can answer most questions you might have."

Liz and Judy spent the next hour walking from one display to another, amazed at what they were seeing. Liz felt like she'd stepped into a different world – a very vivid world, but one where spells were cast, and evil invoked. She didn't know who was behind the things that had been deposited on Nicole's doorstep, but she couldn't help but shiver thinking that, based on what they'd seen in the last hour, there was a good chance they were involved in Nicole's death.

Liz walked over to the young man behind the counter in the gift shop. "Excuse me, sir. I wonder if you could help me."

"Sure, can. What do ya' need?" he asked, smiling broadly.

Liz opened her purse and took out the dolls and the piece of paper. She looked up at the man. His smile was gone and in its place was the unmistakable look of fear.

"Ma'am, where did you get these?"

She told him about Nicole and then about the pouch Cody had found on his doorstep a few hours earlier. She ended by saying, "I don't know anything more than what I've told you, but since I was coming to New Orleans, I thought maybe I could find out something."

"Them dolls are voodoo dolls. Fact someone pinned a name on one of 'em tells me they wanted to harm the person who got it, and from what ya' told me, looks like they did. The pouch ya' described with them things in it is a symbol of black magic we call gris-gris. The word bacalou with the skull and crossbones is normally used when someone's tryin' to break up a love relationship. Kinda' like a voodoo curse. Does that help ya'?" he asked.

"Somewhat. I know very little about the relationships of the lady who was killed. And since she was murdered, I'm concerned about the man who found the pouch I told you about on his doorstep. I really don't know where to go from here. Do you have any suggestions?"

"Lemme' tell ya', if'n a friend of mine showed me them things and tol' me about the gris-gris, I'd be goin' to a gris-gris doctor fast as I could. One of 'em might be able to help ya."

"I wouldn't have a clue where to find one," Liz said, "and even if I could find one, I wouldn't know what to tell them. Can you help me?"

"Sorry, ma'am, ain't allowed to recommend anyone. Manager tol' me it's got somethin' to do with liability. Guess if somethin' happens to someone and they say we referred somebody, we could be sued. Jes' ask around. Lotsa' people go to gris-gris doctors. Bet someone where you're stayin' might know 'bout one. Been popular here in the local Creole communities forever. All ya' need to do is find a Creole person. They can get ya' one."

Liz started to put the dolls back in her purse, along with her phone which had fallen out of it. When she touched the phone to put it back in her purse, the screen lit up and she noticed the young man staring intently at it. Liz looked down and saw it was the photo of Maddie, Judy, and her that Gertie had taken when they were at the diner having lunch the day before they'd left.

"This is just a photo that was taken yesterday of my friend over there and a woman we were having lunch with," Liz said as he continued to stare intently at the photo. After a moment, she asked, "Is something wrong?"

"Dunno'. Jes' thinkin' it's kind of weird."

"I'm sorry," Liz said. "I'm not following you. What's weird?"

"Weird is that woman was in here 'bout a week-and-a-half ago. She was askin' all kinds of question about spells and mojo, things like that. Had a bad feelin' 'bout her, so I tol' her we were getting ready to take inventory, and I couldn't sell any of the voodoo dolls we have here. 'Bout then some people came into the shop, and I excused myself. She was gone when I finished up with them."

"You must be mistaken," Liz said. "I'm sure Maddie wasn't in New Orleans. She probably just looks like the woman you're talking about."

"No, ma'am. That be her," he said, pointing at the image on the phone, "I'll tell you that. I never forget a face. People 'round here know me for that. Some kind of thing I got from mother. She never forgets a face either. That's her, all right. With everythin' you just told me 'bout, you might wanna' be careful, yerself'."

"*See, what was I telling you?*" the voice in her head piped up.

"I gotta' go." He turned to the man who had walked up to the counter and said, "Help you, sir?"

"Liz, what are you going to do now?" Judy asked as she and Liz started to walk back to the cooking school.

"About Maddie or the gris-gris doctor?"

"Either one. That guy must be mistaken, although it does make me nervous that Maddie told me it would have to be a short lunch, because she'd just gotten back from her vacation, and she was way behind at work."

Liz looked at her. "I can't believe Maddie had anything to do with this. She seemed very sincere about everything. Surely, the man back at the museum made a mistake. If he didn't, that means Maddie could be a suspect, and I find that too hard to believe."

"Stranger things have happened. Things aren't always what they seem," the little voice said.

Judy stopped and motioned across the street. "Look, Liz, there's Marie Leveau's House of Voodoo. Let's go in and look around. Might be something different than what we've just seen." They spent the next twenty minutes looking around but didn't find it to be much different than the voodoo museum.

When they were on the sidewalk and headed back to the mansion, Liz said, "Anyway, as to the gris-gris doctor, I have no idea. I brought my iPad here, but I don't think there would be a number of them listed on the internet, and even if I could find one there, I'm not sure they'd be very trustworthy. I guess if I'm meant to go to one it will happen."

Liz opened the front door of the mansion and had only taken a couple of steps up the stairs when she saw the maid who had brought them the pralines and sweet tea the evening before. She was dusting the furniture in the large living room. Liz stepped back down the stairs so quickly she almost ran into Judy.

She walked over to the maid and said, "Good afternoon. I wanted to thank you again for bringing us the pralines and tea yesterday. They were wonderful. I'm sorry, but I don't remember your name."

"Afternoon, Ms. Lucas, Ms. Rasmussen. My name's Martine." She continued to dust.

"Martine, may I ask you something?"

"Of course, ma'am."

"Are you Creole?"

"Yes, ma'am. My whole family is. Come from the Cane River area up in Natchitoches Parish. Why?"

"Well, you saw some things in my room last night that caused me to go to the Voodoo Museum. I showed them to a young man who worked there, and he advised me to find a gris-gris doctor. It's against the museum's policy to give referrals. He suggested that I find a Creole person and see if they could refer one to me. Can you?"

Martine's eyes widened. "Ms. Lucas, this be powerful stuff. Don't think you know what you're messin' with. My uncle's one of the most powerful gris-gris doctors alive, but it's a long way up there, 'bout four hours."

Liz had a feeling she was supposed to meet Martine's uncle, whatever it took. "I guess I could miss dinner tomorrow night and drive up there. I'd have to rent a car, but that's not a problem. Do you think he could see me?"

"Ain't got no idea. I'll call him and find out. You go on up to your room, and I'll call him when I'm done in here."

Less than an hour later there was a knock on Liz and Judy's door. Liz walked over and opened it. "Come in, Martine. I hope you have good news to tell me."

"Ms. Lucas, you must be lucky. My uncle has a meetin' with a 'portant businessman in New Orleans tomorrow afternoon. He said he can meet with you about 4:00 at Café Due Monde. It be world famous." She gave a shy smile. "We got good beignets here at the

Richarde House, but they got better. I tol' him you'd be there. Also tol' him what you looked like."

"Thank you so much for arranging this. Martine, can you tell me what to do? I've never done anything like this. What does he charge? What should I ask him? Do I take the things to him or just tell him about them? I feel like a babe in the woods."

"Everybody 'round here calls my uncle Jean Baptiste. He gots a last name, but no one knows it. You jes' call him that. Take the things I saw last night in your room to him and tell him about the gris-gris. He'll probably do some chantin' and might even give you somethin' to give to the man. What he charges? Don't really know. I hear he gives it away if the people are poor. But a rich person like you? Probably 'bout $50 or so. That help?"

"Yes, very much, and here's something for helping me. I really appreciate what you've done." Liz said as she handed her an envelope with cash in it.

Martine pushed it back at her without looking inside. "Ms. Lucas, I can't take this. Helpin' guests is my job."

"Well, you've more than helped me. You've saved me hours of time trying to find a gris-gris doctor. This can be our little secret. I won't tell anyone."

"Thank you, Ms. Lucas," Martine said, taking the envelope and closing the door behind her as she left the room.

CHAPTER THIRTEEN

The next afternoon, promptly at 4:00 p.m., Liz and Judy each ordered a beignet and a cup of coffee from the beautiful barista with the caramel colored complexion and then carried them out to a wrought iron table and chairs in the sun-filled courtyard of Café Due Monde.

"Judy, I don't want to get off on the wrong foot with Jean Baptiste," Liz said nervously. "I better get him a cup of coffee and a beignet as well. I'll be back in a minute."

Just as she was returning to the table, an elderly grizzled black man with tightly coiled white hair peeping out from under the hat he wore walked up to her and said, "You Ms. Lucas?" he asked.

"Yes, you must be Jean Baptiste. I got a cup of coffee and a beignet for you. Please join us." She nodded towards the table. "This is my friend, Judy Rasmussen.

"Well, thank you, ma'am. Don't mind if I do," he said, sitting across the table from them. Liz pushed the coffee and the beignet over to him along with some napkins the barista had given her.

"Martine tells me a friend of yours is dead and another gots a problem. Thinks maybe I can help. True?" the grizzled old man said, before picking up the beignet and taking a bite out of it.

"I don't know if you can help, but yes, that's true," Liz said as she took the dolls and the paper out of her purse. "One was put on my friend's doorstep a few days before she died. Another was put in her locker at a fitness center and this doll was next to her body when we found her. She was murdered." She handed them to Jean Baptiste.

The old black man stopped chewing on his beignet and looked at them. He made a subtle movement, and even though the movement was quick, Liz would swear he had just crossed himself. From the expression on Judy's face, Liz was certain she thought the same thing.

"Missy, dese are bad, really bad. Tell me everything you know 'bout dese things."

"I told you so. I knew it was dangerous. I pleaded with you not to get involved and now it's too late," the little voice said.

Liz told him everything from the moment the doll had fallen out of Nicole's purse at the fitness center to when Martine had called him.

"I know it's too late for my friend, Nicole, but can you help the man who found the gris-gris on his doorstep?"

"Yes, but since you be carryin' dese things, gotta protect you too. The spirits tell me someone has cast a spell, and a woman was murdered. They also sayin' that the gris-gris be 'bout breaking up some love thing. He got a love thing goin'?"

"He did, but the woman who was murdered was the woman he was going to marry."

"Well, looks to me like someone don't want him to live either. Whoever done it must know somebody from 'round here, 'cuz looks to me like someone sure knows about voodoo, and this here's where most of it is."

"That could be. I simply don't know. You said I had to be protected as well. How will you do that, and how can you protect him when you've never met him?"

"Gotta trust me. Spirits'll tell me what to do. Stayin' wid my son here. He a New Orleanian and gots an altar. Need one so's I can make gris-gris bags for you and yer' friend. Here." He passed her an unused napkin that was tucked under his plate. "Use this napkin to wipe yer' brow and these scissors to cut off a little piece of your fingernail. When ya' finished with dat, pull a couple of pieces of hair outta' yer' scalp and give 'em all to me."

Liz and Judy stared at him in disbelief. Liz looked around to see if anyone was watching them, but the only eyes on hers were Jean Baptiste's.

He leaned closer to her. "Ms. Lucas, no need to ask me why. Jes' do it. Spirits know what they doin'."

Unable to believe what she was doing, a few moments later Liz handed him her hair, the napkin, and the end of a fingernail.

"Now when you get back home, call yer' friend and tell him to do the same," Jean Baptiste instructed her, "only he gotta' put it in the bag I'll give ya' fer him. Need to make yer' gris-gris bags in front of an altar. Like I tol' ya', my son's got one."

"Can't do it here cuz I need the four elements. He gots 'em. Tomorrow my boy will bring you two bags. I'll put four stones in each of them. Spirit will tell me which ones. Tell yer' friend not to put anything else in the bag. Need seven things, no more, and you'll be givin' me the other three. Won't work if it's an even number. When I'm at the altar tonight, I'll be casting a spell for each of ya', a special gris-gris spell that'll keep ya' both safe. Here's the thing though. Won't keep ya' safe forever. If another spell's cast against either one of you, might overtake my good spell. Ya' need to find out who be doin' this and why. How much longer ya' gonna be here?"

"We're leaving in a couple of days," Liz said. "Do you think that will be soon enough?"

"Miss, ya' don't know how powerful these bad spirits are. Whoever's doin' it to yer' friend knows plenty. Sure was plenty enough to kill one person. Think if it was me, I'd be leavin' tomorrow. I'll have the gris-gris pouches brought to you early in the mornin'."

Liz looked doubtful. "Do you really think it's necessary that I leave before I finish the cooking school I'm attending here in New Orleans?"

"Lady, don' know nuttin' 'bout some cookin' school, but I sure knows 'bout gris-gris. Ya' stay here and cook, jes might be yer' last meal. Yeah, go home. I'm gonna' give you my phone number. Let me know what happens. Might be able to do a coupla' more spells if need be."

"Jean Baptiste, please excuse me, but I know nothing about you and now you're telling me I need to change all of my plans. I guess I need to know a little more about you."

The old man chuckled. "Sure, Ms. Liz. Don't know of nobody in my family that weren't involved in voodoo. I learned it at the knee of my granny. She 'tol me once that our family was meant to help people and voodoo is our way. I got quite a reputation in Louisiana, and I even baptize people in the faith. We call it the 'lave tete'. All the people bein' baptized in the voodoo faith, that's what we call it, wear white. They bring offerins' to honor Marie Leveau. You mighta' heard of her. High Priestess of Voodoo."

Liz nodded, fascinated. But what followed caused her heart to quicken. "Darnedest offering I ever saw for the ceremony was when one of the women I was baptizin' changed her name to Marie Leveau. Poor thing wanted to be like Marie, but she's just a wannabe. Has a practice not far from where I practice, but it's just so-so. 'Tween us, don't think she's ever been able to make anything happen with what she calls her magic, but some people go to her. Takes all kinds.

"So yeah, Ms. Liz, been doin' this all my life, and I promise that my magic is strong. Ask around and a lot of people will tell you it's the strongest. Hate to say it, but I'm pretty well-known in these parts. Get called down here to New Orleans a lot to help people. Get asked all the time to move down here, but I like it up in Natchitoches Parish. Know it's poor, but I think poor people need my magic more than rich ones. They gotta' believe in somethin', cuz they sure ain't got no money." He stood up and tipped his straw hat. "Nice meetin' ya."

"Wait, I haven't paid you. How much do I owe you?" Liz asked, reaching inside her purse.

"Nuttin'. Sometimes the spirits tell me not to take money. This be one of them times. Good luck."

When he was out of hearing distance, Judy leaned across the table to Liz. "Are you thinking what I'm thinking? That the woman he was talking about was Nicole's sister? I mean wouldn't that be a small world?"

Liz stared back at Judy. "I think this whole voodoo world is small, and I'd bet it was her. If it was, that pretty much eliminates her as a suspect, because her magic wouldn't be strong enough to murder someone. Plus, it sounds like she's really immersed in the voodoo community, and I just don't see her murdering her sister because she's lost weight. Doesn't pass the smell test."

"What is the smell test?" Judy asked, wrinkling her nose.

"I read the term in some book. It just means something doesn't ring true. Kind of like it doesn't smell good, you probably shouldn't eat it or cook it."

Judy said, "You've got a point there. What I'm really struggling with is the museum guy saying he recognized Maddie. If for some unknown reason she was the one who was in his museum shop, and I can't come up with any logical reason why it would be her, that means Cody could be in danger."

"I couldn't agree more. When we get back to the mansion, I'm going to give him a call. He may think I'm crazy, but I'd rather him think that than find out he'd been murdered and I didn't make the call."

"Judy, are you up for leaving tomorrow?" Liz's heart was still pounding, as she tried to shake the voice from her head. "I'm having a hard time wrapping my mind around this. I mean, this upends everything we've planned. And I have no idea how I'm going to explain to Roger I'm coming home early because a gris-gris priest told me to."

"*You better take his advice and go home. I'd bet the reason Jean Baptiste wouldn't take your money is because you're tainted by this*," the voice said, *and he doesn't want anything from you until he casts his spells and does his woo-woo magic. Told you not to get involved. Now people won't even take your money, and that's a first.*"

CHAPTER FOURTEEN

Liz and Judy returned to the Desiree Richarde mansion and immediately walked over to the door that had the sign, "Office" on it.

"Come in," the heavily accented Southern voice said. The woman, Celia Brisson, who had given the instructions and itinerary for the cooking school the first night was seated at an inlaid French partners' desk. Liz remembered seeing one in a home decorating magazine years ago and had been captivated by it. A woman's face was painted on an oval ceramic piece set into the top border of the desk.

Liz could only imagine what something like that would cost if it were for sale. From what she'd seen the last two days, every piece of furniture and every painting in the mansion was from the time the house had originally been built, in the mid-19th century, although she knew the house had been thoroughly renovated several times to upgrade the plumbing and electrical. Even the guest rooms had Wi-Fi.

"Hello, I'm Liz Lucas, and this is Judy Rasmussen. We're going to have to leave unexpectedly tomorrow morning. We don't expect a refund. We just wanted you to know that we've been more than pleased with the accommodations and the school. It's been wonderful, and I'm sure both of us will be preparing the dishes we've learned how to make here. You see, we each own a spa-hotel in

California and serve breakfast and dinner to our guests."

"What an interesting concept," Celia said, straightening her glasses. "Do you do themed dinners?"

"No, but I'm sure we could start with some of the Cajun and Creole dishes we've prepared here."

"Well, my home's here in New Orleans, but this cookin' school's owned by the organization I work for. Celia handed Liz a brochure. "We have schools all over the world and cook in incredible homes that have state of the art kitchens. The people who own the homes are only inconvenienced two or three times a year, and they're well-compensated for the inconvenience.

"Many of our students have been to several of our schools. If you enjoyed this one, you'd probably like the others. I'm partial to one we hold at a beautiful vineyard estate in Tuscany, as well as the one in Singapore. It's part of an incredible compound. I hope you'll think about attending one or more of them. Here's my card as well, and if you have any questions, please feel free to give me a call."

"Thank you. Should we make arrangements for a taxi or will it be easy to get one tomorrow morning?"

Celia smiled. "Darlin', you're in the French Quarter. You can't take two steps without seein' a taxi. Won't be a problem, trust me."

"Thanks. We need to go up to our room and make our plane reservations. Thanks for your hospitality and good-bye."

"Bye, darlin'. Y'all come back, hear?"

They made their airline reservation for mid-morning, and Judy predictably opted for first class. Jean Baptiste had told Liz it was very important for Cody to get the items his son was bringing to her tomorrow as soon as she possibly could. She called Cody to tell him about the latest developments and see if he could come by the lodge the next evening.

He answered the phone on the first ring. "Liz, I'm so glad you called. When I left for work this morning, there was a cross on my sidewalk made of damp salt. I've never seen anything like it. I swept it into the grass, then ran the hose on it. I'm afraid that much salt will kill the grass."

Liz heard the little voice yelling that crosses of salt mean there's danger for whoever lives there. I'm glad you're not going to his house. Be sure he comes to yours.

"Cody, I've decided to come home early, and I'd like to see you as soon as possible. I own the Red Cedar Lodge and Spa. Could you come there tomorrow evening after work?"

"Sure. I've been by it several times, so I know where it is. What did you find out? This is getting scarier and scarier. I thought Nicole being murdered was the worst, but now I'm afraid I'll be next."

Liz didn't want to let him know she shared his fears for his safety. "Cody, just hang in there. I'll tell you everything tomorrow night. I met with a man who's going to help you. I know this is going to sound really strange, but I need you to get a paper towel or napkin and wipe your brow with it when you're perspiring. Go out in the sun if you have to. I also need you to cut off a piece of your fingernail and pull a couple of strands of hair out of your scalp. Bring those three things with you when we meet tomorrow."

There was a long pause on the other end of the phone. "Liz, are you sure I'm going to be okay?"

"Yes, as sure as any of us can be about anything. I have to go. It's time for dinner. See you tomorrow."

CHAPTER FIFTEEN

Roger answered his phone on the first ring. "Well, that makes me feel good. I know my name must have popped up on your screen, and if you're answering the phone on the first ring, you must miss me and want to talk to me," Liz said, laughing. She realized it was the first time she'd laughed all day.

"I'm so glad you called. It's lonesome without you. How's the food in New Orleans? Are you and Judy enjoying yourselves?"

"Very much. I think I've already gained ten pounds. It's been a wonderful experience. Can't wait to fix some of the dishes for you that we learned to make in the cooking school."

"Liz, it's too bad you're there, because I got a call from your son, Jonah, this morning. He called the house and got the answering machine and then he called your cell phone. Evidently you had it turned off. He's coming into town for one night only, tomorrow night. I told him I'd take him out for dinner, and that I was looking forward to seeing him. He's renting a car, so we decided to meet at the lodge. Too bad you won't be here. He'll be gone by the time you get back."

"Uh, Roger, that's why I'm calling. Judy and I are flying home tomorrow morning. I'll tell you all about it when I see you. I saw that Jonah had called, but I haven't had a chance to get back to him.

That's great. We can go to that steak place he likes. It's one of Jonah's favorites. A man by the name of Cody Evans will be coming over, probably just before you and Jonah arrive. He was Nicole's, that woman I told you about, fiancé. I'll fill you in on all the details when I get home."

Roger let out an exasperated sigh. "Liz, what have you gotten yourself into? Why do I have a sense I'm not getting the whole story here? And why do you have to see this Cody guy as soon as you return? What's going on? Are you and Judy in some sort of danger?"

"No, Judy and I are fine. It's a long story, and it's getting a bit complicated. Let's just say I'm learning a lot about voodoo, and I think there's a good chance it was very much involved in the death of Nicole Rogers. I'll tell you all about it tomorrow night. I'd tell you now, but I don't want to miss my last dinner here. See you tomorrow."

*****

Knowing this would be her last Cajun-Creole meal in New Orleans, Liz decided she'd taste everything, so she could recreate some of the dishes when she got back home. She hadn't been at all disappointed in the school. Each student had been given a recipe for everything that was served during their stay, and she knew she'd be referring to them a lot.

The inviting fire in the fireplace warmed the large living room where the appetizers and wine were being served. The afternoon outing had been a tour of nearby plantations which the guests were raving about. Liz was sorry she'd missed it, and she could tell Judy was too. She took a glass of the offered wine and tried the herb and cornbread cakes that were served with a remoulade sauce. *That's one recipe I'll definitely have to try. My guests would love these*, she thought.

"Can't wait to go to that Voodoo Museum tomorrow," the soft southern voice said from where she was sitting at the end of the couch. Liz turned around in her seat so she could talk to the woman.

"I went there this afternoon," Liz said, "and it was fascinating. I learned a lot. I understand voodoo is still practiced here."

"Sure is. I live about four hours from here, and I can tell you that voodoo is very much alive and well in most areas of Louisiana, especially here in New Orleans. It's not even a belief; it's just a part of our life. We use spells for everything, good and bad. We learn early on the things to avoid and how to protect ourselves from them. Of course, we all know the one thing you can't protect yourself from is a dead black cat being in your path."

"What are you talking about? That stuff is all mumbo-jumbo. Also looks like a lot of people are getting rich off of selling these voodoo things to gullible people," the dark-haired man who clearly loved to eat said. The jowls on his chin wagged as he spoke with his mouth full of the mini savory crackers that were laid out in bowls which were spaced around the room. "I mean, think about it. In today's world, do you really think anyone believes that stuff? From what I hear it's nothing more than old wives' tales and witchcraft."

"Well, not gonna' argue with you," the woman said, "jes' tellin' you if you ever see a dead black cat in your path, better find a gris-gris doctor real fast. Woman across the street from us walked out to get her paper one mornin' and there was a dead black cat in her driveway. She died the next day. Sir, some things jes' is. Don't need no intellectual explainin'."

The room was pin drop still as everyone in the room was intent on hearing what she was saying about voodoo. It was a very opportune time for Martine to announce that dinner was being served in the dining room. And what a dinner it was – one that Liz knew she'd remember the rest of her life. It was absolutely exceptional and over the top.

The Desiree Richarde mansion had a large garden in the back yard beyond the courtyard. Fresh fruits and vegetables from the garden were served at every meal and tonight was no exception. A bright green frisee salad with a warm bacon dressing started the meal followed by classic French onion soup prepared in the Creole fashion with spicy herbs and freshly made croutons along with slices of crusty bread.

I should stop right here. I'm full and anything else I eat will go directly to my belly and hips, Liz thought, immediately forgetting about it as the waiters brought in the entrée – shrimp étoufée over grits with collard greens. *I wonder where I can get collard greens in Northern California. This is a first and absolutely not a last! The étoufée and the rest of it I can do, the collard greens – may have to substitute something else.* The meal ended with bananas foster crepes.

The students pushed their chairs back from the large mahogany table which shone from years of daily waxing. The light from the large teardrop chandelier hanging over it had been dimmed. After several glasses of wine and sated from dinner, in the soft light everyone looked wonderful. It was evident that the students were thoroughly enjoying the cooking school. Friendships were made and food devoured – who could ask for more?

I could ask for more, Liz thought. *I could ask that I never see a dead black cat in my path. I hope this whole voodoo thing ends pretty soon. It's beginning to make me nervous.*

Martine pulled Liz aside as she left the dining room. "Got a call from Jean Baptiste a few minutes ago. His son's gonna' bring some things here for you tomorrow mornin' 'bout seven. I'll bring 'em up to you. He's says to tell you to be very careful and call him if you need him. Here's his phone number." She handed Liz a folded piece of paper.

Liz tucked it in her pocket. "Thanks, Martine. I really appreciate your help. See you in the morning."

"*Good thing you're going home,*" the little voice said. "*You tell Cody you can't help him. Give him the gris-gris pouch and tell him goodbye. When a gris-gris doctor tells you to be careful, you better listen.*"

CHAPTER SIXTEEN

The next day the Delta Airlines pilot easily landed the big jet Judy and Liz had flown in at the San Francisco airport. They easily found their luggage and rode the shuttle bus to the long-term parking lot. A little over an hour later they pulled up in front of the Red Cedar Lodge and Spa. Judy walked to her cottage, and Liz walked into the lodge, glad to be home.

There was a message from Jonah on her answerphone telling her he'd be there about 6:15. She opened the sliding glass doors in their apartment that overlooked the ocean and began to air out the downstairs. *Better call Roger and tell him I've arrived safe and sound.*

"Hi, Roger. I'm back at the lodge, safe and sound. I touched base with Jonah, and he'll be here about 6:15. What time do you think you'll be here?"

"Count on about the same time, unless I get stuck in a traffic jam leaving the city. Missed you and I'm really looking forward to seeing Jonah. It's been too long."

*****

Promptly at 6:00 there was a knock on the door. Liz opened it and looked at Cody who was standing there, looking disheveled. "Cody, have you gotten any sleep?"

"Liz, I can't sleep. I can't eat. To be honest, I'm a nervous wreck, and I'm scared to death," he said, walking into the great room of the lodge. "I don't think I'm very good company right now. I've found out a lot of information and none of it makes me feel any better."

"Well, tell me quickly, and I'll ask questions later. My son and husband will be here in a just a few minutes. Here's a pouch a gris-gris doctor prepared for you. It should help. You need to put those things in it that I told you about on the phone. Now tell me what you found out."

Liz listened intently, understanding why Cody was having trouble sleeping and eating. Nothing he said made her feel any better about the situation.

"We'll talk more tomorrow. Looks like my son and husband just drove up. Try and get some sleep. I'll call you in the morning."

*****

The hostess at the steak house just outside of Red Cedar seated Liz, Jonah, and Roger at a window table overlooking the ocean. Jonah was the first to speak, "Mom, how was the cooking school? I know you were in New Orleans, but that's about all I know."

Liz looked at Roger, silently sending him a message to say nothing about voodoo or black magic. He winked, acknowledging the unspoken message. She turned to Jonah, "It was wonderful. The people are so gracious and the food – well, the next few dinners I prepare at the Red Cedar Lodge are definitely going to be based on Cajun – Creole cooking. The food was everything food should be.

"The school was located in the French Quarter in a magnificent old house called the Desiree Richarde mansion. It was really something. It looked like you could get everything from cheap Mardi Gras beads to really high-end antiques in the French Quarter, and it's still as beautiful as it must have been in the 19th century."

"I'm glad you enjoyed it, Mom, but why did you come home

early? Roger told me you weren't coming back until later tomorrow."

Liz tried to keep her voice light and cheery, although having just seen the state Cody was in weighed heavily on her mind. "That was the original plan, but a couple of things came up here that I needed to tend to. Nothing important, but I thought they better be taken care of."

Liz thought she'd gotten away with it, but when they were finished with their meal, Jonah pushed his knife and fork together on his plate and leaned across the table to squeeze her hand. "Mom, I may have inherited a little bit of your ESP powers, because I would bet about everything I own that you're not telling me something. What's going on?"

"If I felt it was something I needed to tell you about, I would. You'll have to trust me on this, Jonah. It was time for me to come home. I'm fine. We can talk about this later." She looked up at the waitress who had walked up to their table. "I can't speak for the two gentlemen, but I would like some coffee. Would you both care to join me?"

"Mom, I'll have a coffee, but you haven't heard the end of this. Are you sure you're all right?"

"Yes, I'm sure."

"Like I said, Mom, this is not the last you're going to hear of this. I'll be back in a minute. I promised a client I'd call him. It won't take long."

When Jonah was out of earshot, Liz turned to Roger. "Did you tell him anything?"

"Not a thing. What would I tell him? Quite frankly, I don't know anything, anyway, he's just very perceptive. Rather doubt he got to such a high-level position without being perceptive, but I definitely think you owe him the courtesy of an explanation. He's obviously sensed something. Who knows? He might be able to help. And quite frankly, I'd like to know what's going on as well."

"The last thing I want to do is involve you or my son in some voodoo thing," she said. "I'm really tired. Why don't you pay the bill, and I'll go find Jonah? He can have a cup of coffee when we get home."

Roger had just finished paying the bill and was putting his wallet back in his pocket when he heard Liz scream from outside the restaurant. He ran to the door, opened it, and saw Jonah and Liz staring at the ground.

"Roger, get a trash bag from the waitress and bring it out here." Liz said with an urgent tone in her voice.

Moments later Roger joined Liz and Jonah who were standing next to Roger's car. Jonah had pushed Liz behind his back. "Mom, just stay there. I'll take care of this. Roger, would you please hand me the trash bag?"

"Jonah, what's going on? What do you need it for?" Roger asked.

"Looks like some poor cat chose the space next to your car as the place for it last breath. I'll get rid of it."

"Wait, Jonah," Liz asked. "What color is it?"

"It's black. Why does that matter?"

Roger took two steps over to Liz and put his arms around her, feeling her body quiver. "Liz, what's wrong?"

Liz could barely get the words out. "I'll tell you when we get home."

A short while later the three of them were sitting in the lodge's great room, Liz visibly shaken by the sight of the dead cat. Jonah was the first to speak. "Mom, what does it mean?"

"I don't know who it was meant for. Possibly me. The people in New Orleans are pretty superstitious, and dead cats are very high on their superstition list. They believe it's an omen of danger, or worse yet, death, for the person whose path it's in. I think someone is sending me a warning."

"I knew it, Mom, I just knew it. Tell me everything," Jonah said, glaring at her.

Liz spent the next hour telling Jonah and Roger everything that had happened, even what the woman at the cooking school had said about black cats. She also explained about the gris-gris pouch she'd given Cody just as Roger and Jonah had arrived at the lodge earlier that evening. When she finished, there was silence, each of them deep in thought.

"I suppose the good thing is that Cody didn't find one. Hopefully, he's done what he was supposed to do and the spell the gris-gris doctor prepared for him is working," Liz said.

Roger had been very quiet and then he said, "Liz, you know how hard it is for me to believe any of this stuff, but maybe you better call the gris-gris doctor tomorrow and tell him about the black cat. Maybe he can do a spell for you or tell you something you can do. I'm really concerned, and this is something I know nothing about."

The little voice interrupted him and said, "*Liz, get over to Cody's house now. He gave you his address. Take Roger and Jonah with you. Do it! You'll never forgive yourself if you're too late.*"

CHAPTER SEVENTEEN

Liz stood up suddenly. "Roger, Jonah, come with me. We don't have a second to lose. We've got to get to Cody's before it's too late. Hurry," she said, half pushing and dragging them out the front door.

"One sec, Mom," Jonah said, running into his bedroom. He returned almost immediately with his jacket on.

"Roger, you drive. I have his address. Let me get directions to his house off the GPS on my phone."

"Mom, what is going on?" Jonah asked. "What made you decide we have to go there right now?"

"Jonah, remember me telling you about the little voice that tells me things? We've talked about it before. Well, it was very adamant that we get to Cody's right now, or it might be too late."

Jonah looked out the back window and to the sides. "There's no one following us, and I guess that's a good thing. Should we call the police?"

"Yeah, and say what? That a little voice told your mother to go to someone's home because of a dead black cat, a pouch, some wet salt, and a note. Oh yeah. Knowing Seth, I'm sure he'd make that a priority," Roger said sarcastically.

"Mom, there's something I better tell you," Jonah said. "You know how I always travel in a private company plane? Well, that's because I'm always armed, and I wouldn't be able to get through security if I flew on a commercial flight. My job is really high paying, but there's a down side to it. I'm a target in a lot of the places in the world, and the company I work for is always worried that it might extend to safer places. The reason I'm telling you this is because I didn't want you to come unglued if you ever saw a gun in my hand."

Liz raised a hand to her chest. "Jonah, you never told me that. I thought your job was perfectly safe, and that you simply traveled to different financial institutions all over the world."

"Little more to it than that, Mom. We can talk about it some other time. Think we need to make this guy Cody our number one priority at the moment."

"Roger, from the addresses I'm seeing on the houses, he must be in this block." Liz glanced up from the GPS on her phone and gestured out the window. "There, that's got to be his house, the one with the porch light on. I recognize his car from when he was at the lodge earlier."

Roger pulled over to the curb, and they rushed out of the car and up to the front door. Roger banged on the door. Jonah reached under his jacket, and Liz saw the gun in his hand. Just then they heard Cody's raised voice. "Who is it?"

"Open up, Cody. It's me, Liz."

In a moment, the door swung violently open. "Oh, thank heaven you came. Someone, I'm sure it was a woman, had her arm wrapped around my neck and was trying to strangle me."

"Which way did she go?" Jonah asked, interrupting him.

"Out the sliding door to the patio. When you knocked on the door, she released me," he said, his voice shaking with fright. Liz put her arm around Cody and led him to a couch in the front room.

Roger and Jonah headed for the patio. Jonah bent down and took a second gun, a small pistol, from inside his sock and handed it to Roger. "Do you know how to use this?" he asked Roger, as they scanned the patio and the grassy area behind it.

"It's been a while, but yes. Looks like his backyard slopes down to a street. You take the right side, and I'll take the left."

They walked down the slope to where it ended at a street, but they saw nothing. Both of them scanned the area to either side and in front of them. Jonah motioned for them to return to the house.

"Let's go room to room. Maybe whoever it was opened the slider as a ruse," Roger said. Several minutes later they returned to where Liz was sitting with Cody. "Whoever it was is gone. Are you all right, Cody?"

"Yes, but I'm very, very lucky. I don't know how someone got in. I have an alarm system, and I know I set it before I went to the lodge earlier."

"Well, you can't stay here tonight. Go pack a bag and you can stay in one of my cottages. We had a cancellation earlier, so there's an empty one and the lodge is very secure," Liz said. "I have an excellent guard dog that you can take to your cottage and have him stay with you. Believe me, nothing bad happens when Winston is with you. And if you should hear him growl, just call me at the lodge. From the guns I see in both Jonah's and Roger's hands, I think all of us will be safe. Even if you called the police, I don't think there's much they could do."

Roger spoke up. "Cody, I'm going to call an attorney in my firm who specializes in criminal law. Liz has had dealings with him before, and he understands about her whatever it is, the knack she has of a little voice warning her of danger. Maybe if you and Liz could meet with him and tell him everything, he could come up with something. I can't promise anything, but it's a place to start."

"All right. Let me pack a bag. I've got a dog, but she's a sweet little girl, not a guard dog. She was probably licking the hand of whoever it was. She'll be okay to stay here by herself. I've got a doggie door for her, and I'll come back in the morning to feed her."

Jonah walked behind him to his bedroom, gun drawn. "Know it looks a little melodramatic, Cody, but you've had enough surprises for tonight."

Roger took out his phone and called Matt, one of his partners at his law firm in San Francisco. "I know it's really late, but I need your help. Liz has managed to get herself into another situation, and I wondered if you could come to the lodge first thing in the morning." He was quiet for a moment. "Thanks. Here's the address. See you then."

He turned to Liz. "Matt has friends in the police department and elsewhere that can run some computer checks on some of the people you told us about. He's also going to get in touch with Sean, the private investigator I use at the firm.

"I know you trust Sean, and he's been a huge help to you in the past. It might help us figure out who's a possible suspect and who isn't, plus you and Cody will only have to tell your story once. By the way, Matt respects your whatever after it saved the lives of all of those people in Bellingham, Washington."

"Tell him everything. You and Cody need all the help you can get. I told you not to get involved, and now it's too late. If it hadn't been for me, Cody would be dead. In the morning call Jean Baptiste and ask him to cast a spell on whoever put that dead black cat next to Roger's car."

CHAPTER EIGHTEEN

Matt Jones was at the lodge at 8:00 a.m. the next morning. He parked his car, got out and shook Roger's hand. "Matt, I don't think you've ever met Liz. This is her son, Jonah Lucas, and this is Cody Evans, a friend of Liz's. Come on in and make yourself comfortable."

A few minutes later, Matt said, "Please tell me everything that's happened, so I can get an idea of how I can help, and trust me, as a criminal attorney I've heard it all."

Cody told him what had happened to him during the last few days, concluding with the interrupted assault that had occurred the prior evening. He also told him everything he knew about his murdered fiancée, Nicole. When he was finished Liz told him what she and Judy had found out when they were in New Orleans, including her meeting with Jean Baptiste and the gris-gris pouches he'd made for them. Matt listened, making notes from time to time.

When they stopped talking Matt said, "Liz, you mentioned your friend, Judy. Will she corroborate what you've told me?"

"Yes. The reason she's not here is that she had to leave when we returned to get back to her hotel and spa in Calistoga. She felt she'd been gone long enough. Going to New Orleans with me was a spur of the moment thing."

"Okay, I'll call her if I need to. Cody, you mentioned that Nicole had a sister, and there was also a woman she'd fired. I think that's a good place to start."

"Yes, but I don't think either one of them is a viable suspect." Cody went on to outline what Liz already knew from Judy. "Nicole and her sister were estranged. She once told me that her sister legally changed her name to Marie Laveau, you know, the woman who was known as the voodoo queen in New Orleans. She said her sister had really gotten into voodoo. She wondered once if she and her sister had become estranged because Nicole was so fat, and her sister, Marie, was so beautiful. She thought Marie might have been embarrassed to have a sister as fat as she was."

Liz interjected, "Before you go on, Matt, let me tell you what I heard about what Marie's been up to." She told him about her conversation with Jean Baptiste and how Marie was practicing voodoo.

"Okay, bear with me," Matt said. "I may have to interrupt from time to time. Let me get this straight. She said she hadn't seen her sister for years, and Nicole thought they might have been estranged because she was so fat. Was she?" Matt asked.

"Not when I met her," Cody said. "She told me once she'd lost a lot of weight. She said she and her sister really didn't have any mutual contacts who might tell her Nicole had lost weight, so she probably didn't even know that Nicole had transformed her appearance and become quite beautiful. She mentioned that their mother was deceased."

Matt fired off more questions. "Was she on Facebook? Did she post pictures there? Did anyone take her picture that you know of? I'm trying to figure out if there is any way her sister might have found out about the weight loss."

Cody shook his head. "She told me once that she was leery of those social network things and that she wasn't on Facebook. The only time she mentioned anything about pictures of her was when her bank did an article on her weight loss. She was pretty embarrassed about it. She said it was entitled something like 'If This Top-Notch Bank Employee Can Do It, So Can You!' She mentioned the bank was having some type of a health promotion for their employees. She said she'd felt like she was nothing more than a poster child, and it wasn't a very good feeling. She said she hadn't wanted to do it, but the bank had been pretty insistent."

"Do you know if it got picked up by any other media? And Cody, are you talking five pounds overweight or more?"

"I don't know. It wasn't something Nicole liked to talk about. She felt she'd dealt with it, and it was in the past," Cody said.

"I think I can answer that," Liz said. "Judy and she belonged to the same fitness center here in Red Cedar, and Judy told me Nicole had told her she'd lost one hundred fifty pounds, so it was a lot more than five pounds."

Matt scribbled in his notebook and turned back to Cody. "You mentioned something about Nicole firing someone. What was that about?"

Cody told Matt about the woman Nicole had fired when she'd become the bank manager and how it had worked out in the woman's favor.

"Matt, that's the same thing that Maddie Sanders, the woman who was Nicole's assistant manager told me. I think both her sister and the employee are dead ends," Liz said.

"Okay, it looks like we can rule out both of them. Cody, I understand that you and Nicole were going to be married. Had she been seeing anyone else before you started seeing her? Say someone who would have been angry because the two of you had apparently developed a serious relationship?"

"Not to my knowledge," Cody said. "She told me once that she felt like she was in junior high instead of being a successful thirty-year-old bank manager, because people normally didn't have their first dates at that age. I took that to mean that she hadn't dated, and if she was that overweight, there was probably some truth to it. She was the real deal. We loved each other. It was that simple." His voice was breaking up, and he stood up and walked over to the window. Liz noticed him wipe what looked like a tear off his cheek.

"Cody, I'm sorry to ask you all these questions, but believe me, it's necessary, so we don't waste precious time on irrelevant things. This is pretty obscure, but what about you? Were you seeing anyone before you started dating Nicole? Would someone want to get back at you by murdering Nicole and then scare you. I see the look in your eyes, but people get real funny about things, and this could be a reason."

"Yes, there was someone, but I haven't seen her since I started seeing Nicole."

"All right. Give me her information."

Cody told him about Candace, where she worked, and how he had broken up with her. He told Matt he'd had no communications with her since then.

"Well, I think that's about all we can do for now. Let me see what I can find out." Matt turned to Liz. "I'm not a big voodoo fan, but I don't think it would hurt for you to call this gris-gris doctor in Louisiana and have him do some mumbo-jumbo. Looks like someone wants to make life pretty difficult for Cody. Liz, Roger, if it's all right with you, I'd suggest Cody stay here for a couple of days until we get a handle on this."

"That's fine with me," Liz said. "As I mentioned to Cody last night, we had a cancellation, and the cottage he was in last night will be vacant for the next couple of nights."

She turned to Cody and said, "Winston was with you last night, but I also think Winston should be with you at all times until this gets solved. Even at work. You can put him in your office, and he'll be fine."

At the sound of his name, the big boxer, who had been sleeping on his bed in the corner of the great room, walked over to her. Liz put his head in her hands and said, "Winston, go to Cody. Stay with him for now. Be on guard."

Liz had always suspected he understood English, because he went over to Cody and sat down next to him. Liz called Bertha and told her Cody would be staying in the cottage for a few days.

"Okay, Cody. Bertha is setting it up for you. Take a little time for yourself. As you know it's quiet here. There aren't any televisions in the cottages, but there is Wi-Fi. I doubt you slept much last night, and I think right now a nap would be the best thing for you. There's a refrigerator in the cottage, and it's well stocked. Dinners are here at the lodge. Unless something comes up, I'll see you tonight. Winston, go with Cody," she said in a commanding voice.

When they were gone, Liz said, "Matt, I didn't want Cody to hear this. He's got enough on his mind, but I need to tell you a couple of things. The first is that I have a photograph of the woman he'd been seeing before Nicole." She told him of her conversation with Gertie and showed him Candace's photograph. The voodoo doll could clearly be seen in the photograph.

Matt picked up Liz's phone and spent a lot of time looking at it. "Liz, would you email this to me? I definitely want to find out more about this woman. Here's my email address," he said as he handed her a business card. "What else do you have for me?" he asked as he returned her phone to her.

She spent a moment emailing him the photograph of Candace and then continued, "I told you about the conversation I had with the man in the museum gift store, but I omitted part of the conversation." She told Roger, Matt, and Jonah about how the man had seen the photograph of Maddie and was certain she'd been in the shop a week earlier.

All three of them were speechless when she finished. Roger was the first to comment. "Liz, you and Judy had lunch with Maddie. What was your gut feeling about her?"

"I thought she was very forthright, and I felt she was honestly grieving over Nicole's death. If it hadn't been for my conversation with the man in New Orleans, I never would have thought twice about her. I mean, she was the one who got me in touch with Cody."

Liz looked down at her phone and said, "I suppose it would be a long shot, but maybe she wanted to be the manager of the bank. Maybe she was the one who murdered Nicole, although I find that a real stretch. But even so, from what I understand, she didn't even know Cody, so where does an attack on him and the voodoo things he's received fit in? It makes no sense to me. Maybe it's two people, but it's pretty hard to believe that there would two people in the little town of Red Cedar who wanted to harm people by using voodoo."

"I agree, but it certainly seems significant. You said the man in the store saw a photo. Was it on your phone?" Matt asked.

"Yes, here it is. I'll send it to you. It was a photo of Judy, Maddie, and me, which was taken by Gertie. Those are the two things I was talking about."

"Okay, you've definitely given me some food for thought on the drive back to the city." Matt turned to Jonah. "Let's err on the side of caution. I'd feel better knowing that you were keeping that gun with you. Let's hope you don't have occasion to use it, but I'll feel better if it's close by. I'll call you as soon as I know anything. Liz, try not to worry. You've done a great job and given me plenty to work with."

*****

After Cody had gone home to feed his dog, he decided to forget work. He returned to the lodge's cottage, took a nap and when he woke up he'd come to the lodge. He was sitting in the kitchen watching Liz and Gina prep the food for the dinner that was being served at that lodge that evening when Liz's phone rang. "Liz, it's

Matt. May I speak with Cody?"

"Sure, just a moment. He's sitting here talking to Gina and me while we get ready for tonight's dinner."

"This won't take long," Matt said.

Liz handed the phone to Cody and said, "It's Matt." She continued the preparation, and a few minutes later Cody returned her phone to her.

"Liz, thanks for your hospitality. I really appreciate it. Matt said he'd hired a bodyguard for me. He'll be staying at my home until this is resolved. Matt said he's used him a number of times before, and he trusts him completely. He did tell me he thought it would be a good idea if I took Winston with me, if you don't mind."

While they were talking, Jonah walked into the kitchen with his suitcase in his hand. "I heard that, and I think that's a good decision, you'll feel much safer with a bodyguard. He turned to Liz. "Mom, be careful. I'd stay if I could, but I have an important meeting I have to attend. I'm worried about both you and Cody. Maybe you should get a bodyguard, too."

"No. I'll be fine. We're pretty secluded here, and Roger will be here at night, as well as Bertha and her husband, plus all of the guests staying in the cottages. I don't think there will be any problems here. I'm so glad you could come, even if it was just for one night."

"Love you, Mom," he said, kissing her lightly on the cheek. "I'll be calling and checking in on you. Good luck, Cody. I'll be thinking of you," he added as he turned and walked out the door.

*****

As soon as Jonah got in his car, he called Roger's law firm and asked for Matt. "Matt, it's Jonah Lucas. I'm worried about Mom. I just heard you got a bodyguard for Cody. If you think Mom needs one, I'll pay for it."

"No, and that's one reason I wanted Cody to be away from your mother. I'm pretty sure Cody is the target, not your mother. I think the black cat incident was because Cody had been at the lodge just before the three of you went to the restaurant. I imagine someone had been following Cody but didn't want to risk being seen driving onto the lodge property. I'd bet whoever it was thought he'd gone with you to the restaurant. I promise if anything occurs that makes me think otherwise, I'll hire one in a New York minute. Okay by you?"

"Thanks, man. I really like Roger, but I haven't been around him all that much, and I have no idea if he can protect her if he needs to. I'm leaving on a trip, and I won't be around to lend a hand if he needs it."

Matt laughed. "Trust me. Roger would do everything in his power to protect your mother. He absolutely adores her. I really don't think you need to worry about it. When I left the lodge earlier today, I took some time and looked around. There's only one way in and out and certainly enough people around that I don't think anyone would try and harm Liz."

"I trust your judgement, but please keep me in the loop."

"Will do and have a safe trip."

CHAPTER NINETEEN

"May I speak to Jean Baptiste?" Liz said to the young woman who answered the phone with a heavy Southern drawl.

"Jes' a minute. I'll get him."

A few moments later a man's voice said, "This is Jean Baptiste. How may I help you?"

"Jean, this is Liz Lucas. We met two days ago. You said to call if I needed you, and I think I do." She told him about the dead black cat and the assault on Cody.

"Both of you need a spell. I wish you were here, but my grandson tells me what a computer whizz he is and says he can send things by computer. Let me have your email address, and I'll cast a spell for you and your friend. Johnny can send them. What's your email address?"

Liz gave it to him. "Is there anything else I can do until we find out who's doing this?" she asked. Liz wanted to make sure she had all the bases covered. If Jean Baptiste had told her to run naked through Red Cedar, she would have considered it if she thought it would help find the murderer.

"You and yer' friend be sure and have your gris-gris pouches on you at all times. Don't have to be around your neck. They can be anywhere on your body. 'Portent thing is that they're on your body. They'll protect you."

"Thank you, Jean Baptiste, I really appreciate your help."

"Yer' welcome. Funny thing happened. Had a call a little while ago from some woman who lives in Northern California. Said she needed more powerful magic than she'd been usin'. Said she tried to use magic to break up a relationship, but it hadn't worked, so she needed something stronger. Said she'd been to a gris-gris doctor, but his magic hadn't worked. Tol' her I don't do black magic. Kind of a coincidence, don't you think? You and yer' friend bein' from Northern California and all."

"I think that's beyond coincidence. Did she give you a telephone number?"

"She did but can't find it right now. If I do, I'll send it to that email address of yours. Probably nothin', just kind of strange is all."

"Yes, very. Thanks again, and I'll look forward to hearing from your grandson."

She got off the phone and called Cody, filling him in on what Jean Baptiste had said about the gris-gris pouches. The next call she made was to Matt. "Matt, I'm sorry to bother you, but the more I think about this, the stranger it is." She told him about her conversation with Jean Baptiste and what he'd said about the woman who had called him.

"Liz, give me his number. There's a little-known device that one of my men uses that can trace a phone call after a number has been called. I'll call this voodoo guy and see if we can make it work."

She gave him Jean Baptiste's number. "Oh, Liz, one more thing. Your son is very worried about your safety and wanted to hire a bodyguard for you, but I'm certain the only reason the dead black cat was left next to Roger's car was because Cody would be in the car.

This has nothing to do with you. If I felt otherwise, I'd arrange for protection for you."

"Thanks, Matt. I appreciate it. Please, let me know what happens."

*****

Her phone rang late that afternoon. "Liz, I have good news and bad news," Matt said. "We were able to trace the number from Jean Baptiste's phone. That's the good news. The bad news is that we traced the call to a pay phone in a restaurant in Red Cedar. Some place called Gertie's Diner. Ever heard of it?"

Liz audibly gasped. "Are you kidding, Matt? It's practically an institution in our town and in this part of Northern California. It's even a stop for people on bus tours, and the owner is a friend of mine. Jean Baptiste told me that the call was made this morning. Does that jibe with what your guy found out? Do you have a particular time?"

"Give me a minute. He wrote it in an email. Here it is. It was made at 11:47 Pacific Standard Time. Think you can find anything out about it?"

"I'll call my friend right now and get back to you. There's a pay phone at the restaurant in the hall where the bathrooms are located. Let me see what I come up with." Liz ended the call and pressed in Gertie's name on her phone.

CHAPTER TWENTY

A moment later Liz heard the aging icon on the other end of the line. "So how was The Big Easy?" Gertie asked. "Bring me some of them pralines I asked ya' to get me? And aint' you home early? Ain't seen Handsome today, that gorgeous husband of yers', so didn't know ya' was back. Comin' in today with my pralines?"

"Let me start by saying The Big Easy was wonderful, and I do have pralines for you. I can't come in today, but Roger can give them to you tomorrow. And yes, I am home early. Do you have a minute?"

"Fer' you, darlin', I got all the time in the world. What's up?"

Liz told her everything that had happened since she'd last seen her, knowing that even though Gertie knew everything that was happening in Red Cedar, if the situation called for it, she could be the soul of discretion. She left out the part about Jean Baptiste's conversation regarding the phone call he'd received and Matt tracing the call. She planned on asking Gertie about it, but she wanted her answer to be spontaneous.

"Well, don't that beat all. So, yer' thinkin' it might be that woman we saw in the photo with the voodoo doll. Would I be right?"

"Yes, I am. I'm also a little concerned about the woman Judy and I had lunch with at your place, Maddie Sanders. The gift shop owner was adamant that she'd been in his gift shop the week before."

"Be more inclined to think it was the woman with the voodoo dolls. Got a name for her?"

"Yes, it's Candace Norgan. She was the pretty blond."

"I 'member, Liz. May be gettin' up there in years, but the brain is as young as it's ever been. Matter of fact, saw her jes' before lunch."

"You saw Candace today?" Liz asked, her heart speeding up, wondering if she could have been the one who called Jean Baptiste.

"Sure 'nuf. Took her order myself. Wanted to see if she had any more of them voodoo dolls, but she didn't put any on the table this time. After I took her order she asked if I had a phone that guests could use. Said she had to make a phone call and her cell phone weren't workin' right. Kinda wondered when she said that, 'cuz I woulda' sworn she was lookin' at it when I walked up to her table."

"Gertie, this is really important. Do you know if she used the public phone, and if so, about what time?"

Gertie was uncharacteristically quiet for a moment, then she said, "Liz, why are ya' askin'?"

Liz told her about her conversations with Jean Baptiste and Matt. "That's why I'm asking, Gertie."

"Yes, she did use the phone, although I ain't got no idea who she was talkin' to. One of the waitresses tol' me there was a problem with the sink in the women's restroom. Ya' gotta' know just how to jiggle it sometimes to unplug it, so I passed her in the hall when I went there. When I walked out she'd finished. As fer' time, have to be around 11:45, 'cuz we got two busloads of customers 'bout then, and we were jammed until 1:30. Does that help?"

"More than you know, Gertie, more than you know. Thanks. The pralines will be there tomorrow."

Liz called Matt back and told him about her conversation with Gertie. "Matt, it looks like Candace was the one who called Jean Baptiste. You know, he was very explicit that the woman had said she was trying to break up a relationship. I'm no defense attorney or law person, but that sure doesn't shout murder to me. Do you think that's all she's trying to do, break up a relationship? Maybe she doesn't know anything about Nicole's death. Maybe it was someone else."

Matt was quiet for several moments and then said, "Could be a case where two and two doesn't equal four. Maybe she's not the murderer, although that seems hard to believe. I guess it's possible someone wouldn't know about the murder if they didn't watch television, read the paper, or know someone who knew the victim. It's a long shot, but I think it should be explored."

Liz racked her brain. "I honestly don't know what to think. I think I mentioned in one of our conversations that she owns an insurance agency. Maybe she's been on vacation or leave and doesn't know what's happened. I suppose that's possible."

"Let me look into it. I'll get back to you."

Liz put her phone on the kitchen counter and saw Gina looking sideways at her. "It's none of my business, Liz, but are you involved in solving another murder? Does this mean I'll be hosting some of the dinner parties in the near future?" she asked referring to several times when Liz had left her in a lurch while she'd been away catching the bad guys.

"Yes, I am, and I have no idea what will be happening next. I wish I could tell you more, but I don't know more," Liz said with a frown. "I'm dealing with a bunch of voodoo stuff, and I think I may be in way over my head."

Gina walked over to her and put her hand on Liz's arm. "Please Liz, whatever I can do, just let me know. I'm perfectly capable of handling the lodge dinners when you have to be gone. That is one thing you definitely don't have to worry about."

Liz put her hand on top of Gina's. "Thanks, I really appreciate that. I'll try not to leave you in a lurch, but as you well know, sometimes it becomes necessary for me to leave rather quickly."

CHAPTER TWENTY-ONE

Liz had just reached the bottom of the stairs when Roger walked in the door that led to the parking lot. "Hi, beautiful, how is the voodoo queen doing? I talked to Matt a little while ago. He'd never used Sean before and asked what I thought of him," Roger said referring to the private investigator at Roger's firm that Liz had used several times in the past.

"What did you tell him?" Liz asked as she put her arms around him and drew his head down, lightly kissing him.

"I told him I thought he was the best. Matt has always used another private investigator at the firm for his cases, but that guy is on vacation right now. He said to tell you that he'd have something for you within the hour." True to his word, just as he finished speaking, Liz's cell phone chimed with the song Roger had entered, "I Left My Heart in San Francisco."

"Liz, it's Matt. I have some interesting information for you. I found out that Candace Norgan has been on vacation for two weeks and will be off another week. This muddies up the case, but there's an outside chance she's not the murderer and may not even know that Nicole has been murdered. Maybe when she called Jean Baptiste she was being honest when she said she was trying to get something to break up a relationship."

"Matt, quite honestly I don't know what to think about that. It just seems too odd that there would be two people in this small town who have had access to voodoo objects and who would want to harm or kill someone. I mean, I know it's possible, but it sure doesn't seem plausible, if that makes any sense."

"It makes a lot of sense, but I think we need to figure out what to do next."

"I agree." There was a beeping on the line and Liz saw there was another call coming through. "Matt, can I call you back? I see that Cody is calling me, and I probably should take his call."

"Sure."

Liz pressed the green button on her phone screen. "Hi, Cody. I was just on the phone with Matt. What's happening?"

"Liz, this is the strangest thing, but I just had a phone call from Candace. She told me she'd been in touch with someone from New Orleans, and he'd told her that we were meant to be together. She asked if she could stop by and talk to me. She said the person had told her that Nicole was not the right person for me, but that she was."

"Good grief. What did you tell her?"

"I said that I needed to think it over. What do you think I should I do?"

"I was talking to Matt when you called. Let me run it by him and see what he thinks. I'll get back to you in a couple of minutes."

She pressed in Matt's numbers. "Matt, this is getting stranger and stranger. I just heard from Cody. You're not going to believe this." She told him what Cody had said and ended by asking his opinion on what Cody should do.

"Whew. This really is getting complicated. So much for one person carrying out some voodoo thing. It seemed pretty cut and dried until a little while ago. I was pretty sure it was Candace, now

I'm not so sure. Okay, let me think about this."

He was quiet for a few moments and then he said, "I'd like to see Candace go over to Cody's house. If she is the murderer, at least the bodyguard I hired for him will be there along with Winston, your dog. By the way, Roger told me some of the stories about Winston. I had no idea he was that good. I really think Cody's well-being is covered, but I digress.

"I'd like to know if Candace is aware that Nicole is dead. I don't want you there, and I'd certainly have no reason to be there. I think the best thing to do would be for the guy I hired to put a wire on Cody, so I can hear, and you too, if you'd like, what Candace has to say."

"What about Winston?" Liz asked. "I couldn't stand it if something happened to him."

"I don't think that's going to be a problem. I rather doubt she's planning on murdering Cody, since she asked if she could go to his house and talk to him. He can say he's taking care of a friend's dog, and that should be a good enough reason for Winston to be there."

"What about the wire? Does the bodyguard you hired keep one in his car or what?" Liz asked.

"As a matter of fact, he does. Strange things happen in this business, and you always need to be prepared. I'll tell him what to do. I'm going to drive up to Red Cedar. If it's too late for me to make it back to the city, do you have an empty cottage I could stay in?"

"Yes, we're almost always booked solid, but this week we've had a couple of cancellations. You're welcome to spend the night."

"Okay, I'll call Cody and my guy and give them their marching orders. I'll fill you in when I get there. I want to be near Cody's house in case something gets ugly. His bodyguard is going to have to be off premises as well, because that would probably send up all kinds of red flags, whether she's guilty or not. Let's plan on me picking you up, and I imagine Roger will want to be in on this as well, about 7:30. I'll tell Cody to ask her over about 8:00. That should be plenty of time for us to get situated. See you then."

Roger had just walked out of the bedroom, having changed into casual clothes. "What were all the phone calls about?" he asked, scratching his head. "Have I missed something?"

"Matt will be here at 7:30 to pick us up. Let me tell you what's happened, and then I'd like your take on this. You spent a lot of years as a defense attorney. Hope you can give me some insight here on the criminal mind." She started out by telling him about her conversations with Cody and Matt.

Roger sat down in the chair across from her in the small kitchen in their living quarters at the lodge. Behind her the sun was setting on the Pacific Ocean and it looked like fingers of flame were racing across the water. He knew it would only last for a minute, but every time he saw it he thought about how, after his first wife had died of cancer, he'd gotten a second chance at life. And it was a very good second chance.

When she was finished, he said, "I agree with everything Matt is doing. As far as Candace is concerned, obviously it could be one of two things. First, she may legitimately be unaware of Nicole's murder, even though there's all this circumstantial voodoo stuff. Secondly, she may be the murderer and is professing not to know anything, hoping people would think she wasn't involved. Convoluted, but the criminal mind is often not the shortest distance between two points."

Liz chewed her lower lip. "Roger, let's assume for the sake of conversation that Candace was not the one who committed the murder. Do you think there's a chance that Maddie really was the woman the man identified in New Orleans? And if so, what do we do about it?"

"Sure, there's a chance. She did tell Judy that she'd just come back from a vacation, but what bothers me is the lack of a motive. Like it or not, Candace would have a motive, that of a jilted woman. But you haven't told me anything that speaks of motive with Maddie. From what I understand, Maddie didn't even know Cody. Is that correct?"

"As far as I know, yes. But for the sake of discussion, she very well might have known of him. Certainly, she heard Nicole speak about him, and she did mention that Nicole had a picture of him on the cabinet in her office. Who knows? Maybe she had a thing for him, although I grant you that's not much of a motive for murder."

"I agree. What do you want to do about dinner tonight? Looks like we won't be eating with the guests."

"Oh gosh, I need to tell Gina that she'll be front and center tonight. Let's eat when we get back from the stakeout or whatever it's called when you're listening to people and one of them is wired. There will probably be some leftovers from dinner, and anyway, I'm too nervous to eat right now."

"Sounds good to me," Roger said as Liz hurried up the stairs to talk to Gina.

*****

"Gina, I am so sorry, and I can't believe we were just talking about this, but you're going to have be the recipient of the accolades for tonight's dinner. That little matter I'm involved with needs me to be somewhere during dinner. If there are any leftovers, I think Roger and I will have those later tonight. You and I made a lot of Cajun gumbo, and I doubt the guests will eat all of it. Although as good as it is, they just might. Anyway, try and save a little for us."

"Liz, I can practically guarantee you that there will be some left over. As a matter of fact, I'll dish out two bowls right now and put them in the refrigerator for you. That way, Roger won't have to worry. I know how he loves your cooking."

"Correction, Gina, our cooking. And if you could squirrel away a couple of pecan praline bites, that would be great. Knowing Roger's sweet tooth, I think those will make a pretty good impression on him. And who knows how tonight will turn out? Thanks again for covering for me."

"Any time, Liz, any time."

CHAPTER TWENTY-TWO

Liz and Roger had just walked outside the lodge when they saw Matt's headlights coming up the lane that led to the lodge from the highway. He pulled up to them and Roger and Liz got in his car.

"So, what's the drill, Matt? Even though I've done a lot of criminal defense work in the past, this is a first for me," Roger said.

"Several things. First of all, I'm going to wire Cody. Sid, the bodyguard I hired, will be right outside the back door. He'll be listening to everything through a receiver he'll have on him, and we'll be doing the same thing as close as we can get to the house without being spotted. Probably about half a block away. That's the beginning."

"Won't that be a problem when Candace drives up? Isn't there a chance she'll spot us?" Liz asked.

"No, as soon as we see headlights, you two can scoot way down in your seats, and I'll be looking at my phone, like I'm lost. To my knowledge, she's never set eyes on any of us."

"I think that's true. There's no way she would connect people in a car with Cody."

"My thinking, exactly, Liz. I would like you to work with Winston a bit. Roger told me some of the incredible things he can do. I'd like you to instruct him, however you do it, that if Cody is in danger Winston should act to prevent whatever is happening. Can you do that?"

"Of course. He's been exceptionally well-trained. What worries me is how is Cody going to respond to Candace wanting to get back together with him?"

"He and I talked that over while I was driving up here. We finally decided the best thing to do is just let Cody play it by ear. Kind of string her along and then tell her he wants to think things over. We thought that would prevent her wanting to spend the night or something. If there's any chance that she's the murderer, obviously that would not be a good thing."

"What about me, Matt. Need me to do anything special?" Roger asked.

"No. I just want you to be another set of ears. In case we ever have to use this conversation in court or anything like that, I might need you to corroborate what is said. But I need to talk to both of you about something else."

"Sure, Matt. What's that?"

"Roger, I took your advice about your private investigator. Since mine is on vacation, and time is getting away from us with this murder, I called Sean and gave him the information I had on both Maddie Sanders and Candace Norgan. He's pretty amazing. Think I'm going to have to start using him."

"What was so amazing?" Liz asked.

"Within an hour he not only confirmed everything we knew about Candace Norgan, he even found out she hasn't left this area during the time she's been on vacation. He also found out that Maddie was on a flight to New Orleans and stayed there one day. He even gave me the name of the hotel where she stayed and also found out that when she returned to San Francisco, she picked up her car from the parking lot and returned to Red Cedar a week before Nicole was murdered."

"How did he come up with that information that fast?" Liz asked as Matt turned onto Cody's street.

"Credit card information, but I've saved the best for last."

"You're killing us, Matt. What's the best?" Roger asked.

"Maddie ordered a number of things from a web site in New Orleans called Marie Laveau's House of Voodoo."

He was interrupted by Liz, "Oh, my gosh. I was there. It's on Bourbon Street in the French Quarter. After Judy and I went to the Voodoo Museum, we decided to see what it had to offer. It's got voodoo dolls, gris-gris pouches, all kinds of voodoo things. Do you know what she got there?"

"Yes. She bought several voodoo dolls, two gris-gris pouches, and several books. Doesn't say she murdered Nicole, but she sure never mentioned any of that when you had lunch with her at Gertie's Diner. Makes a person wonder. Okay, let's get this over with," Matt said as he got out of the car and Liz and Roger did the same.

CHAPTER TWENTY-THREE

Cody was waiting for them and as soon as he opened the door, Winston ran over to Liz, clearly glad to see her. She knelt down and kissed him on the forehead. "What a good boy, you are," she said, as Winston furiously wagged his short stubby tail acknowledging the praise.

"Liz, if you're ever in the market to sell that dog, I sure would like the right of first refusal. He's something else. My dog is sweet, but Winston seems to know what I'm thinking before I do. I'm sorry all of this has happened, but I'm not sorry I've had an opportunity to spend some quality time with him," Cody said.

Liz whispered in Winston's ear. "Don't worry, big guy. I would never sell you."

A large man walked over to Matt and shook his hand. Matt turned to Roger and Liz and said, "I'd like you both to meet a friend of mine, Sid Moretti. He's the one who's staying here with Cody." The three of them shook hands.

Matt took control. "Okay, Cody, I don't think we have much time. I told you what we were going to do, so let's get started. Liz, while I get the three of us ready, would you take care of Winston?"

"Sure." She knelt down next to Winston and told him exactly

what she wanted him to do, mainly to protect Cody. She stood up and walked over to Cody. "Cody, I'm sure this won't be necessary, but Winston is also trained to protect through hand signals. Let me show them to you, just in case you need them."

Roger looked over at her and smiled. "This reminds me of when Winston protected Michelle when she had to use the hand signals at a doctor's office in San Francisco. Let's hope it isn't called for tonight."

"Agreed," Liz said.

Matt opened a briefcase he'd brought with him and spent the next few minutes explaining how the voice activated transmitter and the receivers worked. Each of them was wired with the appropriate electronic device, a transmitter for Cody and receivers for the other four.

"Liz, I know I told you that Sid had some in his car, but these just came out, and they're supposed to be better than what he has," Matt said.

"Sid, glad to see you have a sweatshirt on. I have no idea how long Candace will be here, but at least you'll be comfortable standing outside. Liz, Roger, it's time to get in the car." They hurried out the front door and down the street to Matt's car. A few minutes later a car drove toward them, passed them, and turned into Matt's driveway. A blond woman was driving.

*****

The woman got out of her car and walked up the steps to the front door. A moment later it was opened and they heard Cody greet Candace. She stepped inside and it was quiet for a moment.

"Cody, thanks for seeing me. I've missed you. I've done a lot of thinking since you came to my office. Mind if I sit down?" Candace asked.

"It's good to see you, too. Please, have a seat. A lot has happened since I last saw you."

"I took some time off, Cody. I had it coming, and I was pretty devastated by your visit and you telling me that you no longer wanted to see me. Even though I've thought about it a million times, I can't figure out what happened."

"Candace, it was nothing you did. I just met someone that I fell in love with. It doesn't mean there's something wrong with you. I didn't ask for it. It just happened."

"Cody, is there anything I can do that would make you break up with this woman, this woman whose name I found out is Nicole Rogers. Anything at all? I don't think I want to go on living if you're going to marry her."

"Candace, I guess you haven't heard. Nicole was murdered."

It was quiet for several moments and then Candace said, "I'm sorry for you, Cody, I didn't know. I've been so devastated by our breakup I haven't watched any television or read the newspapers. How did it happen? Do you know who did it?"

"No, very little is known. It seems to have something to do with voodoo, since she'd received several voodoo dolls and one was found at the scene of the crime. No one knows if those figure into the murder."

"Cody, you don't think I had anything to do with it, do you?" Candace asked in a quavering voice.

"Why would I think that?" he asked.

"Because I was reading that magazine article about New Orleans when you came to see me. Before you came in I'd even ordered some voodoo dolls to enhance our relationship. I promise you I didn't have anything to do with it, and I never gave or sent your lady friend one. I never even met her. The dolls that I ordered were good magic dolls, not bad magic. I understand there's a difference.

"The ones I got said that they had been blessed by a voodoo doctor to make sure that relationships went smoothly. After you left my office that day, I remember thinking I should have sent away for them earlier. By the time I got them, there was no relationship, and I never used them."

"I'm sorry if I hurt you, Candace. I never meant to. Right now, I'm really confused by everything, and quite frankly, I'm hurting."

"I'm sorry, Cody. I probably better leave. I didn't know anything about Nicole, and I can see this isn't a good time for me to be here, but I would like to say one thing. If you ever need someone to talk to, or if you change your mind about our relationship, you have my number. Goodbye, Cody. I wish you well."

"Thank you, Candace, and right now I'm so confused I might regret anything I said. I'll keep your words in mind."

From the sounds they could hear on their receivers, the listeners could tell that Cody and Candace were walking to the door. In a moment it opened, and Candace walked down the steps, got in her car, and left.

"I don't know about you two, but I thought that was pretty sad. She came across as very honest and innocent to me. I'd like to know your thoughts," Liz said after Candace had driven off, and they were sure she wasn't coming back.

"I agree," Roger said. "I didn't hear anything in her words or in the tone of her voice that would lead me to think otherwise. If she did murder Nicole, she's in the wrong profession. She should be an actress."

"My sentiments exactly," Matt said. "I don't see any tail lights, so I think it's safe for us to go in the house. I'd like to know what Cody thinks, since he could see her facial and body expressions."

CHAPTER TWENTY-FOUR

Matt knocked on the door and said, "Cody, please open the door. Candace is gone, and we need to talk to you."

A grim-faced Cody let them in the front door while Sid came in the back door. "Were you able to hear our conversation?" he asked.

"Yes, Matt said. "We won't stay long, but we would like to get your opinion. I'm particularly interested in knowing if you thought her body language matched what she was saying."

Cody sat down heavily in a chair and gestured for them to do the same. "Let me start by saying that I never found anything wrong with Candace. It was just that I fell in love with Nicole. It really was nothing against Candace. I always thought she was a wonderful person until I met Nicole."

He rubbed his hands over his face and said in a voice heavy with emotion. "I honestly don't think she was the one who murdered Nicole. Her movements, her expressions, her body language, everything indicated she didn't know anything about the murder. I could be wrong. Let's face it, this is my first time having anything to do with a murder, but I would bet everything I own that she's innocent."

"All right, Cody, let's assume you're right. I know this isn't relevant to the murder, but do you have any thoughts about what your relationship with Candace will be in the future?" Liz asked.

Cody took a deep breath and said, "No. I have absolutely no idea what will happen. We cared for each other deeply at one time. From what she said, I think she still does. Can I ever care for her in the same way again? I honestly don't know. Plus, if I was her, the thought would always be in the back of my mind that it might happen again, and quite frankly, I don't know if I could guarantee her it wouldn't, and that would not be fair to her."

"Cody, I've gained quite a little wisdom from being on this earth for more than a few years. And the one wisdom I've learned from experience is that time is a great healer along with listening to your heart." Liz gave him an encouraging smile. "Sometimes our brains try to make sense of things or sort them out in what is commonly thought of as a rational matter, but the heart never lies. When your heart has healed enough to speak to you, listen to it."

Liz stood up and said, "Matt, Roger, I think it's time we left Cody alone. He needs some time. Sid and Winston are here, so I think he's in good hands. Cody, I'll talk to you tomorrow. Try and get some sleep." She walked over to him and gave him a big hug. "You remind me a lot of my son, Jonah, and what I just said would be the same advice I'd give him if he was in your shoes."

Matt and Roger shook hands with Cody while Liz talked quietly to Winston. As they were leaving, Liz asked, "One more thing, Cody, are you planning on going in to work tomorrow?"

Cody nodded. "Yes. I've been away from my clients for too long. I've monitored my email, and I can tell that some of them are getting restless. I can't afford to lose any business."

"Well, in that case, I think I'll come by and get Winston in the morning. What time do you plan on leaving for work?"

"Well, I'm usually in the office by 6:15 in the morning because the stock market opens at 6:30 our time. Let me save you the trip. I'll drop Winston off at the lodge on my way to work. Sid told me he wants to be with me, so I'm going to tell people a relative of mine is in town and wants to see what a typical workday is like for me. I know that's kind of lame, but it's about the best I can come up with for now. I don't know what I'll say if this continues much longer."

"I have a feeling it won't. Let's just get through tomorrow," Liz said as she walked out the door, followed by Roger and Matt. The two men discussed the events of the evening, but no conclusion was reached, other than they tended to agree with Cody's assessment of Candace's innocence.

While Matt and Roger were discussing all of the angles of what was known so far, Liz had come up with a plan that she didn't dare discuss with either one of them, or even Cody. It involved Sean, Winston, and what she preferred to think of as discovery, rather than breaking and entering. She was quiet the rest of the way home, working out the details in her mind.

When they got back to the lodge, the guests had left, and Liz and Roger walked upstairs to have a late dinner. Gina had definitely looked out for them, leaving them both full meals in the refrigerator along with a note which read, "Hope your evening was as successful as the dinner the guests enjoyed. See you tomorrow afternoon."

When they'd finished, Roger said, "I'm beat. Today was my first day back in the office after being in the city for a few days, and I had non-stop appointments. I'm not complaining, I'm just using it as an excuse to go downstairs, take a shower, and head for bed. Looks like Cody will be here bright and early, and I'd hate for Winston to be wandering around, feeling neglected."

"Go ahead. I need to do a few things up here before I join you. I'll be down shortly." She waited until she heard the shower running, then she picked up her phone and pressed in a telephone number.

"Hi, Sean, it's Liz Lucas. I know you stay up late and get up early, so I'm hoping I didn't wake you."

"Nope, just looking at the computer before I head for bed. What's up?"

"I've got a favor to ask. I know you've done some work for Matt on the Rogers case, but I think I know who did it and how to prove it. Any chance you could come to the lodge tomorrow morning after Roger goes to work, say about 9:30?"

"Liz, this worries me. You have a tendency to get into, how shall I put this…let's just say situations that Roger would not like you to get into, and I have a strong feeling this may be one of them. Would I be right?"

"Could be, but if it doesn't work out he'll never need to know about it."

"Since you're probably planning on doing something that is either illegal or dangerous, and you'd do it anyway, yes, I'll be there about 9:30, although I don't like keeping secrets from my employers. Matt and Roger have been very good to me."

"I promise this won't jeopardize your relationships with them," Liz cajoled, "and if I'm right, it will only make them better."

"All right. You're always willing to listen to my problems with the fairer sex, so I guess this is payback time. I do have two favors to ask of you."

"Shoot," Liz said.

"May not have been the best choice of words, Liz. I want you to have your gun ready and Winston by your side. I'll bring my gun as well. Anything else I might need?"

"Yes, bring whatever tools are used to jimmy a lock. One more thing. I need you to get the home address of Maddie Sanders."

She ended the call before Sean could change his mind.

CHAPTER TWENTY-FIVE

Roger was showered, shaved, and dressed by the time Cody dropped Winston off. He could tell that Cody had definitely made room in his heart for the big dog by the way he reluctantly handed his leash over to Roger.

"How are you doing this morning, Cody?" Roger asked.

"Better, now that I've had a good night's sleep. It was uneventful, and that was just fine with me. Sid and I are going into the office, and I'm hoping this nightmare will be over soon."

"I have a feeling it will. With Liz, Matt, and Sean on it, I'd say your chances of getting back to a quieter way of living are pretty good. I'll be in my office here in Red Cedar today if you need anything. Take care," he said as he and Winston walked into the downstairs area of the lodge.

"There you are, Winston. Welcome home. I missed you," Liz said as she petted the big dog and took off his leash. "I don't know if Cody fed you this morning or not, but I don't think having an extra meal will hurt you. Come with me." She walked upstairs to the kitchen and put his dry dog food in a bowl and about a half a can of dog food on top of it. He looked at her as if saying thanks and began to chomp it down.

When she went back downstairs, Roger was standing in front of the mirror, fixing his tie. "Liz, I'm going to the office early this morning. As I told you last night, yesterday was a zoo, and I need to deal with some things before the normal day starts. I should be home about the regular time. What's on your agenda today?" he asked, putting on his suit coat and checking his briefcase to make sure he had everything he'd need for the day.

Liz bent over and busied herself making the bed, so she wouldn't have to look directly at Roger while she was being less than truthful with him. "I want to talk to Bertha and see if I need to do anything for the spa or the lodge. She'd mentioned that she wanted to start carrying a new line of spa products, and she asked for my input. I know we have a full dinner group tonight, so I'll be working on that, too. Why don't you plan on joining us? People always like it when you're here, you know, kind of the king of the realm type thing."

"That was your first error, Liz. I was fine with you not telling me what you have planned for today, but then you went and said something so out of character like me being king of the realm. That's when I knew that you were being less than fully truthful. Now tell me what you really have planned for today." He waited for her to respond, knowing from experience that when Liz was acting like this, he'd be hard-pressed to get a straight answer.

She fluffed a pillow and looked at him sheepishly. "Roger, if I told you I was well protected by a gun, a friend, and Winston, would you feel better?"

"Marginally, Liz, only marginally. When do you plan on telling me about whatever it is you're going to be doing today?" He gave her what he hoped was a stern look.

"Oh, when you get home tonight. It's really nothing. Just a little something I want to check out," she said breezily.

"I can tell by your tone of voice this is a losing battle. All right, just be careful. You know how much I love you," he said leaning down and kissing her. What worried him even more was that

Winston had walked over to Liz and was standing next to her. He'd always thought Winston had some ESP abilities, and if Winston felt she needed protecting, that did not bode well, but he also knew there was nothing he could do.

"All right, my love. I'll see you tonight." He looked down at the big dog. "Winston, this is not a request. This is an order. Guard Liz." He walked out the door with a final wave.

*****

When Roger pulled out of the lodge's driveway and was on the highway leading to town, his cell phone rang. He pulled over to the side of the highway and saw that it was Sean.

"Good morning, Sean. What's up?"

"Roger, I talked to Liz last night, and I thought I better tell you about our conversation. I know she has a tendency to get into situations that can be dangerous, and I think this might be one."

He listened to Sean and when he'd finished, Roger said, "I really appreciate the call. I'll be there. Go on in, and I'll join you. I think Liz might be really angry if I show up before you're in the house. And Sean, thanks for the call."

CHAPTER TWENTY-SIX

Promptly at 9:30, Sean pulled up to the lodge. Liz had been watching for him and she and Winston quickly walked down the steps and got in his car. "Good morning, Sean. Thanks for doing this for me. It shouldn't take long."

"Mind telling me what shouldn't take long, Liz, since I kind of have my head on the chopping block here if something goes wrong?"

"We're going over to Maddie's home. When I had lunch with her a tape recorder fell out of her purse. She said that she'd started dictating the events of her days. I'm hoping to find something that might point to her being the murderer. Did you bring the things you might need to pick the lock?"

"I brought some things, but I assumed they were for you."

"Are you kidding?" Liz asked in surprise. "You're the private investigator. What would I know about picking a lock?"

"Liz, this is not making me feel good. What if she's at home?" Sean asked.

"I'm sure she'll be at work, particularly since there's no longer a branch manager. She told me she'd be filling in until a new one was appointed."

A few minutes later, Sean pulled into a strip mall parking lot and stopped the car. "Sean, there aren't any houses here. Why did you stop here?"

"Because I want to draw as little attention to this caper as possible. If we put my car on her street or in her driveway it would probably be a red flag if any neighbors were watching."

"Okay, that makes sense. What now?"

"You get Winston, and we'll walk around the corner to her house. We'll just look like two people out to take their dog for a morning stroll. The area looks pretty much like a working-class neighborhood, so I would imagine everyone is gone for the day. We'll just walk up the sidewalk, knock on the door, and if no one answers, which I assume will happen, you and I will stand in front of the door, and I'll open it."

"I can do that," Liz said.

"Sure, you can. It will be easy. If anyone is watching us, they'll think we were invited into the house. Okay, are you ready?" he asked as they got out of his car and started walking towards Maddie's home.

"This has got to work," Liz said, keeping pace with Sean's longer strides, "because if it doesn't, I really am afraid someone will do something to Cody, and I've started to think of him as a second son."

A few moments later, they were on the front porch of Maddie's home. Sean easily jimmied the lock on the front door and in less than thirty seconds they were inside the small one-story house. "I'm thinking she would put the tapes that she'd filled either in an office, if she has one, or in her bedroom. Why don't you search the bedroom, and I'll take the office?"

"Will do."

Liz walked into what looked like an office. There was a bookcase, a desk, and a large easy chair with an ottoman in the room. She looked in the drawers of the desk, and the various compartments of it, but found nothing. She walked down the hall to the bedroom and asked, "Any luck, Sean?"

"No, but I found a lot of books and even some large envelopes containing different things that looked like they had something to do with voodoo. I even found instructions on how to use some of that stuff. This looks pretty suspicious to me. What about you?" he asked, "find anything?"

"The desk is clear. I just feel certain she must keep the tapes in one of these two rooms. Let me go back in there and look again."

When she walked over to the bookcase in the office she saw a homemade box on one of the shelves. It looked like someone had made it in a woodworking class. It was oak and had the initials "MR" on it, Maddie's initials.

Although Liz's little voice had been silent for quite a while, it suddenly said, "*You've found it. Open the box, Liz. Open the box.*"

When Liz opened it, she found exactly what she'd hoped to find. Rows and rows of cassettes were arranged by date in the box. She found the one for the week Nicole was murdered and quickly removed it from the box. She'd brought a tape recorder with her, the one she often took to restaurants in case she wanted to remember the way some dish had been prepared or served, and she took it out of her purse.

"Sean, I found what I was looking for. Come in here and listen to it with me." When he walked into the office, she showed him the cassette. The week's date was neatly written in heavy black letters on it. She inserted it into her recorder and they both leaned forward to listen to it.

"Today, I did it. It was so easy. I've been planning this for so long. I thought it would be fitting that Nicole would know that someone was going to kill her because of the voodoo things I planted. The mailbox was a cinch, but the one I put in her desk at work was a little dicey. Miriam walked in just as I was closing the drawer. It was a close call, but I'm sure she didn't suspect anything."

"She did it, Sean. I just knew it had to be her!" Liz said with excitement in her voice.

"Hit play again. Let's see what else she has to say."

Liz pressed the play button. Neither one of them noticed that Winston had stepped between them and that the guard hairs on his back were standing up. They continued to listen.

"Killing her was easier than planting all the voodoo stuff. She was unlocking the door of her house, and I just walked up behind her, put the wire around her neck, and killed her. It was really easy, and it felt good."

"Sounds like she was pretty sick," Sean said.

Liz reversed the tape, and they heard something about Cody. Just then they heard a voice say, "Don't move. I don't have time to mess with any voodoo stuff on you two, but now since you know I killed Nicole, this gun in my hand will be just as effective."

Liz recognized Maddie's voice, and turned around, trying to ignore the pistol pointed at her chest. Her immediate thought was to keep Maddie talking. She knew that Sean carried a gun and so did she, plus Winston was there. Maybe they'd get lucky. "Maddie," she said calmly. "What are you doing here? Why did you murder Nicole, and why were you terrorizing Cody?"

"I came home to get some fresh tapes. I didn't have any more at the office. You're so smart, I'd think you could figure out why I did it. I didn't get the promotion to bank manager, no, they had to bring in that soft-spoken Southern belle from New Orleans. When I found out where she was from, it was only natural that something would happen to her that would be familiar to her, like voodoo.

"As for Cody," she said her voice becoming dreamy, "I've loved him for a long, long time. He gave a talk once at the bank about investments, knowing we dealt with people who had substantial amount of disposable income. It was love at first sight. I couldn't stop thinking about him. I found out everything I could about him.

"I was madly in love with him even when he was seeing Candace. I knew where he lived, where he worked out, what he ate. Everything. I never thought he and Nicole would become serious. I figured she'd just get fat again, and he'd lose interest, but she didn't, and he didn't. I couldn't let her have him. After all, she got the job as manager, was I supposed to let her have him too? No…"

Maddie was cut off by the sound of a gunshot and then the gun she'd been holding in her hand came flying across the room. In one quick movement Sean ran over and picked it up, pointing it at Maddie.

Liz turned and looked at the person standing in the office doorway. It was Roger, with a smoking gun in his hand. He ran over to Liz, holding her, reassuring her that everything was all right. At the same time, he put his hand on Winston and said, "Winston, on guard." He looked at Maddie and said, "If you're having any thoughts about trying to run away before the police get here, forget them. Winston will take you to the ground instantly, and I can assure you it won't be a pleasant experience."

Roger pressed a number into his phone and when it was answered, said, "Seth, this is Roger Langley. I've caught Nicole Rogers' murderer. I'm holding the killer at gunpoint. You need to get over here right away."

"Oh man, Roger, I was jes' finishin' up some paperwork 'bout all those speedin' tickets I've been writin' up. Ya' know the council meets tonight 'bout my raise, and it's a pretty big deal to me."

"Seth, let me put it this way," Roger fumed. "If you aren't here in ten minutes, I will be at the council meeting tonight speaking strongly against a raise for you and then I will begin a recall action against you, and I will run for the office of police chief myself. How does that sound?"

"Sheesh. Don't need to get all testy 'bout it, Roger. I'm on my way."

"Thought you would be, Seth. Make it snappy but be careful. Be a shame if you had to give yourself a speeding ticket."

Liz began to giggle.

EPILOGUE

"I told Gina we needed to take some downtime what with everything that's happened in the last few days, so Gina is taking care of the dinner guests for tonight," Liz said when Roger walked in the door. "Plus, I wanted to try a new dessert out, and since it's a little strange, I didn't think I should beta test it on the guests."

"So, what does that make me, the resident guinea pig?" Roger asked with a laugh. "And just what is so strange about this dessert? I don't recall you doing this before."

"I haven't. Could be the perk or the punishment of being the husband of a lodge and spa owner, but I think you'll be okay with it. The thing is it's an avocado and chocolate tart. I know you like avocados, but I have to admit I've never had one with chocolate. We'll see. To another subject, I know you were going to meet with Matt today. Anything new on Maddie?"

"Avocado and chocolate? You're kidding. I dunno, Liz, that could be really awful or super fantastic. And yes, I did meet with Matt. Maddie pleaded guilty to murdering Nicole, and she'll be sentenced in about thirty days. The probation department will prepare a report and recommend a sentence to the judge."

"Do the judges usually take their advice?" Liz asked.

"Usually, unless there are some really strange circumstances, but I don't see any in this case."

"What kind of a sentence do you think she'll get?"

"Probably life imprisonment. Maybe she'll spend it reading all those books she got on black magic, although in the end it didn't seem to help her," Roger said.

"Why do you say that? Nicole's dead."

"Think about it Liz. Nicole didn't die from some spell or hex. She died because she was strangled to death by a wire wrapped around her neck."

"That's true," Liz said, as she applied the chocolate ganache to the avocado tart. Her phone was on the kitchen counter and it started ringing. "Excuse me, Roger. It's Cody. I called him earlier just to see how he was doing."

"Thanks for returning my call, Cody. I was just calling to see how you are doing."

"I'm doing fine," Cody replied. "The stock market has been in a yoyo mode the last week, so I've been really busy trying to assure investors that it will straighten out, and there's no reason for them to panic."

"I'm glad to hear that. I understand Maddie entered a guilty plea and is up for sentencing pretty soon," Liz said.

"I know. Matt and I have been talking, and he told me if I want to, I could speak at her sentencing about Nicole and the murder, but I've decided to put it behind me. I need to get on with my life."

"Probably a good decision. I've watched those courtroom scenes where the victim's family members speak out about the defendant's sentence, and it always seems to be terribly emotional. If I was a friend or a relative of a victim, I don't think I could go through something like that. Wonder if Maddie will try to use any hexes or spells to help get a lighter sentence. They sure didn't seem to keep her from getting arrested."

Cody was quiet for a few moments and then he said, "I don't know. Maybe there is something to them."

"Seriously, Cody? What are you talking about?"

"Well, I've seen Candace a couple of times. You may remember she bought the dolls and things to cast spells to get us back together. Who knows? Maybe it worked. Liz, I have to go, a new client just walked in. I know I've thanked you before, but again, I don't know if I'd be talking to you now if you hadn't figured out who murdered Nicole. And I'll never forget that I was next on Maddie's list."

"Cody, I wish you and Candace well. It's kind of a different romance story, but maybe some magic is involved. Keep in touch. I'd like to know how it turns out."

"I will, Liz. And thank Roger and Winston for me. All of you saved my life, and I'll never forget it. I hope I can repay you in some way, but let's hope it doesn't involve spells," he said with a laugh as he ended the call.

*****

"Okay, Liz," Roger said. "This is officially a perk. I can say with unreserved enthusiasm the chocolate avocado tart is a success. Matter of fact, I'm going to have a second piece. Murder makes me hungry."

RECIPES

AVOCADO CHOCOLATE TART

Ingredients:
½ cup shelled unsalted roasted pistachios (I could only find salted ones, so I rinsed them with cold water, dried them off with a dish towel, and let them dry for about an hour)
6 oz. dark chocolate wafer cookies (I like the Famous brand.)
2 tsp. sugar
Kosher salt (You'll only use a couple of pinches.)
6 tbsp. unsalted butter, melted
2 medium soft, ripe avocados
8 oz. cream cheese at room temperature
6 tbsp. confectioners' sugar
2 tsp. lemon juice
2 tsp. vanilla extract (Don't use imitation.)
4 oz. dark chocolate (60-64% cacao)
½ cup whipping cream

Directions:
Preheat oven to 350 degrees. Pulse pistachios in a food processor until finely ground. Reserve 1 tbsp. Add cookies, sugar, and salt to the nuts. Pulse until finely ground. Add butter and pulse until mixture is combined. Press into bottom and sides of 10-inch tart pan with removable rim. (I've also used a Springform pan.) Bake 10 to 12 minutes. Place on rack and let cool completely

Scoop the insides of the avocados into the food processor. Add cream cheese, confectioners' sugar, lemon juice, vanilla, and a pinch of salt. Pulse until smooth. Spread filling onto the crust, filling it evenly. Chill while you make the ganache.

Put chocolate in a heatproof bowl. Heat cream in saucepan until bubbles form at the edges. Pour cream over chocolate and let stand 1 minute. Mix until smooth. Cool ganache for 5 minutes. Pour over avocado filling and spread to cover evenly. Sprinkle with reserved finely ground pistachios. Place in refrigerator. After two hours place plastic wrap on top. When ready to serve remove rim. Enjoy!

ROASTED TOMATOES WITH GARLIC

Ingredients:
4 cups grape tomatoes
4 cloves garlic, thinly sliced
2 tbsp. olive oil
Salt and pepper to taste

Directions:
Preheat oven to 450 degrees. Place a piece of aluminum foil on baking sheet. Put the tomatoes and garlic in a mixing bowl. Drizzle with olive oil and toss until evenly coated. Season to taste with salt and pepper, then spread onto prepared baking sheet. Bake the tomatoes in the oven until the skins pop and start to brown, about 15-20 minutes. Serve and enjoy!

PECAN PRALINE BITES

Ingredients:
2 tsp. vegetable oil
5 cups pecan halves
¾ cup brown sugar
½ cup granulated sugar
1/3 cup heavy cream
1 tbsp. vanilla extract (Don't use imitation. It makes a difference.)
1 tsp. ground cinnamon
½ tsp. ground nutmeg

Directions:
Preheat oven to 350 degrees. Lightly oil a 9 x 13-inch baking dish with the oil. Place the pecans, brown sugar, and granulated sugar in a large bowl. Toss to combine. In a separate bowl whisk the cream, vanilla, cinnamon, and nutmeg together. Pour the mixture over the pecans and sugar. Mix well and transfer to prepared pan. Bake for 30 minutes, stirring every 5 minutes. Remove from oven, stir, and allow to cool on a baking rack. The hardened pecan mixture will separate and break into small pieces when you put them on a plate or store them. Enjoy!

NOTE: Very simple. These are addictive!

STUFFED PORK LOIN

Ingredients:
6 slices bacon, roughly chopped
2 apples, peeled, stemmed, and finely chopped
1 shallot, finely chopped
3 cloves garlic, minced (I put a little salt on top. Makes chopping much easier.)
1 tbsp. chopped fresh rosemary
¼ cup chopped pecans
4 lb. pork loin roast

2 tbsp. whole grain Dijon mustard
Freshly ground salt and pepper to taste

Directions:

Preheat oven to 450 degrees. In a large skillet, cook the bacon until crisp. Drain all but ½ tablespoon of fat from skillet. Add apples and shallots. Cook until softened, 4-5 minutes. Add garlic and cook for 2 minutes, then stir in rosemary and pecans. Season with salt and pepper.

Butterfly the pork loin: With a sharp knife, cut along length of pork loin without cutting all the way through. After cutting the pork loin, you should be able to open it and lay it flat, like an open book. Season pork generously with salt and pepper. Spread stuffing over the surface. Roll up the pork loin along with the stuffing, and secure tightly with kitchen twine. Rub with mustard.

Place in a roasting pan on a rack with fresh rosemary sprigs and bake for 15 minutes. Reduce oven temperature to 350 degrees and cook for 45 minutes, basting with the pan juices every 15 minutes. Let roast rest 15 minutes and then snip off kitchen twine before slicing. Enjoy!

Paperbacks & Ebooks for FREE

Go to www.dianneharman.com/freepaperback.html and get your FREE copies of Dianne's books and favorite recipes immediately by signing up for her newsletter.

Once you've signed up for her newsletter you're eligible to win three paperbacks. One lucky winner is picked every week. Hurry before the offer ends!

ABOUT THE AUTHOR

Dianne lives in Huntington Beach, California, with her husband, Tom, a former California State Senator, and her boxer dog, Kelly. Her passions are cooking, reading, and dogs, so whenever she has a little free time, you can either find her in the kitchen, playing with Kelly in the back yard, or curled up with the latest book she's reading.

Her award winning books include:

Cedar Bay Cozy Mystery Series
Kelly's Koffee Shop, Murder at Jade Cove, White Cloud Retreat, Marriage and Murder, Murder in the Pearl District, Murder in Calico Gold, Murder at the Cooking School, Murder in Cuba, Trouble at the Kennel, Murder on the East Coast, Trouble at the Animal Shelter, Murder & The Movie Star, Murdered by Wine, Murder at the Gearhart

Cedar Bay Cozy Mystery Series - Boxed Set
Cedar Bay Cozy Mysteries 1 (Books 1 to 3)
Cedar Bay Cozy Mysteries 2 (Books 4 to 6)
Cedar Bay Cozy Mysteries 3 (Books 7 to 10)
Cedar Bay Cozy Mysteries 4 (Books 11 to 13)
Cedar Bay Super Series 1 (Books 1 to 6)... good deal
Cedar Bay Super Series 2 (Books 7 to 12)... good deal
Cedar Bay Uber Series (Books 1 to 9)... great deal

Liz Lucas Cozy Mystery Series
Murder in Cottage #6, Murder & Brandy Boy, The Death Card, Murder at The Bed & Breakfast, The Blue Butterfly, Murder at the Big T Lodge, Murder in Calistoga, Murder in San Francisco, Murdered by Superstition

Liz Lucas Cozy Mystery Series - Boxed Set
Liz Lucas Cozy Mysteries 1 (Books 1 to 3)
Liz Lucas Cozy Mysteries 2 (Books 4 to 6)
Liz Lucas Super Series (Books 1 to 6)... good deal

High Desert Cozy Mystery Series
Murder & The Monkey Band, Murder & The Secret Cave, Murdered by Country Music, Murder at the Polo Club, Murdered by Plastic Surgery, Murder & Mega Millions

High Desert Cozy Mystery Series - Boxed Set
High Desert Cozy Mysteries 1 (Books 1 to 3)

Northwest Cozy Mystery Series
Murder on Bainbridge Island, Murder in Whistler, Murder in Seattle, Murder after Midnight, Murder at Le Bijou Bistro, Murder at The Gallery, Murder at the Waterfront

Northwest Cozy Mystery Series - Boxed Set
Northwest Cozy Mysteries 1 (Books 1 to 3)
Northwest Super Series (Books 1 to 6)

Midwest Cozy Mystery Series
Murdered by Words, Murder at the Clinic, Murdered at The Courthouse

Midwest Cozy Mystery Series - Boxed Set
Midwest Cozy Mysteries 1 (Books 1 to 3)

Jack Trout Cozy Mystery Series
Murdered in Argentina

Coyote Series
Blue Coyote Motel, Coyote in Provence, Cornered Coyote

Midlife Journey Series
Alexis

Red Zero Series
Red Zero 1, Red Zero 2

Newsletter

If you would like to be notified of her latest releases please go to www.dianneharman.com and sign up for her newsletter.

Website: www.dianneharman.com,
Blog: www.dianneharman.com/blog
Email: dianne@dianneharman.com

Made in the USA
Middletown, DE
21 July 2018